WAVE

For the surfers—of water, of words, of songs, and of hearts,
who take the drop into an ocean of stars to reveal the light we are.
—D.F.

Text © 2022 Diana Farid
Illustrations © 2022 Gotobean Heavy Industries, LLC

Rumi poems originally published in *The Essential Rumi*, translated by Coleman Barks
(San Francisco: HarperCollins, 1995). Used with permission of the translator.

Book design by Melissa Nelson Greenberg
Edited by Summer Dawn Laurie
Copyedited by Penelope Cray

Library of Congress Cataloging-in-Publication Data available.
ISBN: 978-1-951836-58-0

Printed in China

10 9 8 7 6 5 4 3 2 1

CAMERON KIDS is an imprint of CAMERON + COMPANY

CAMERON + COMPANY
Petaluma, California
www.cameronbooks.com

WAVE

DIANA FARID

art by Kris Goto

cameron kids

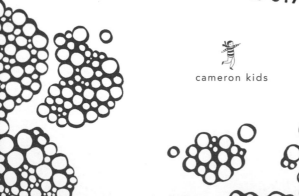

The ocean takes care of each wave
till it gets to shore.[1]
—Rumi

Waves

Swirling blue-green
       seaweed-laced

   W   V   S
     A   E

          U R
        T   N

             C
             R
             A
             S
             H

               F   I   ZZ

I ride

on a wall

of **water** as it plays

tug-of-war with the moon.

I tumble

under

white bubbles and **light** rays

into the sea as it slides toward sandcastles.

Every scent

is seasoned

with salt and **breath**

lost then caught.

Dare

the ocean to dance and it'll

flow

flip

throw

me back,

tease with swells, so I keep

watching

waiting

hoping

for the bigger **wave**,

that might take me all

the way to

the **shore**.

I set a book of Rumi's poetry
on the Haft-Sīn[2] table setting.

Maman wrote in the book,
English translations
of some of the poems,
as a way to practice English.

>   *Ava, don't do that!* Maman fusses.

>   *It should be*
>   *a book of poems by Hāfiz.*
>   *Make a wish. Open the book.*
>   *The page you open to*
>   *holds the answer.*

I'm sunburned from surfing.
The only wish I am making is to eat.

Maman, my uncles, and my aunts stress over
      sweet, slivered carrots and orange-peel rice with chicken,
      dill rice with lemon-soaked salmon,
      a stew of greens, dried limes, and tender steak,
      another stew of ground walnut, pomegranate syrup, and chicken,
      fresh mint, basil, scallions, and feta, ready to be folded
      into warm lavāsh bread.

---

1. Farsi for "new day"; Persian and Bahá'í New Year. (The romanization rules were used selectively throughout the book.)
2. A display of seven items traditional to the celebration of Persian New Year, corresponding to the Northern Hemisphere's spring equinox.

If there aren't leftovers, you didn't make enough.

I'll have to wait to eat
at least an hour, probably two,
after the invitation time.

I open the book of Rumi's poetry.
Wish that, for once,
a Persian party would start on time.

He answers,

There's hidden sweetness in the stomach's emptiness.[ii]

Mihmūnī (a Persian Party)

Everyone has arrived at the party
two hours late.
Right on time for
Persian time.

Every chair in the house
lines the living room walls
for guests to sit.

Coffee tables in the middle,
piled up with fruit, cucumbers, nuts,
and nougat candy,
will get pushed to the side
after dinner
for the eventual dancing.

Phoenix is missing the party.
He and his younger sister, Bel,
have their guitar recitals.
They're not Persian anyway.

I can see his house
from the

     living

          room. Wish I was there listening
          to Depeche Mode and the

     Cure,
not Persian songs
played on synthesizers.

How to Pass Persian Tea

In Iran, girls pass tea.

Maman passes
a large silver tray to me.

Twenty full, delicate, glass teacups,
a bowl overflowing with rock sugar.

The tea is burning hot,
like the jokes
Uncle Rāmīn is telling.

While I hold the tray of teacups out,
I can hear Maman's voice in my head:

Girls who offer tea
with grace,
are thought to,
one day,
make a good
wife.

I move from
one person to the next,
wait as

each guest chooses a glass,
decides if they will take
a piece of sugar.

The tray is heavy,
like the stares of the women
dressed in Armani, Burberry, and Coach.

They lean into each other,
while they watch me
at my own kind of recital.

I'm not the kind of girl for their sons.
(Not that I want to be.)

Maybe because I wear a Billabong T-shirt
and white miniskirt,

maybe because of Maman's divorce,

but today,
they'll take tea from me anyway,

then look in another direction.

Before So Cal

I'm here, and not
      in Iran

because Maman dreamed
of doing her medical training
in New York
in the late 1960s,
when the Beatles ruled the music scene
and miniskirts ruled
      her closet.

She came

      before
      headscarves were law

      before
      Iran would have a revolution

      before
      my uncle was declared a heretic
      for practicing his religion

      before
      his head was draped,
      neck noosed, chest shot

      before
      my grandfather saw bodies hanging in city streets

      before
      he packed the photos, heirlooms, books,
      hid them in the basement
      thinking he'd be back again

before
the revolutionary guard shut the airport down
the day after he got out on a plane

I'm here, and not
          in Iran

because Maman came
to learn how to care for other mothers,
to learn how to deliver babies.

I'm here, and not
          in Iran

because Maman came,
and then had her own baby,

          before her country took her childhood home,

          before she could never go back and be free,

          before
          she knew
          she would stay.

When You're an Only Child

All those two-or-more-player games:
Monopoly, Candy Land, Sorry,
even Hungry Hungry Hippos,
don't need to be.
It's me against me.

That couch with the high armrests,
fuzzy brown and tufted,
is a vault and I'm Nadia Comaneci
going for a perfect 10.

TV is a loyal friend,
concerned that our house is clean.

TV makes sure I have the latest
blond Barbie.

TV tells me about
family dinners around a table
that happen next door, for sure,
like on the frozen-food commercials.

I don't need to share my toys or
fight over what radio station is on.

Maman says:

>   *You are lucky.*

But sometimes,
a lot of the time,
I'd rather not pretend
to be two different players.

Singing in My Bedroom

I've finally memorized
"Lean on Me,"
fingers sore from pressing
rewind and play
on the boom box,
checking how to time the lyrics
like Club Nouveau.

I close my eyes.
I rock on the stage.
I fall with the song
into the hollow
of the wave,
as it covers me with its curl.
We ride the barrel toward the light.

Phoenix

In our kindergarten graduation photo,

I'm the one with the dark brown bowl haircut,
olive skin, and deep-set eyes.

He's the one with golden-orange hair,
freckles, and eyes that squint when he laughs.

But I don't remember playing with him
until our first-grade beach field trip.

My sandcastle was taller than all of the others.
He came over to help me make it taller.

I needed it to be even on both sides.
Three scoops of sand from the blue bucket, left side.
Three scoops of sand from the red bucket, right side.
Three pats after each pour. Start over if it's not right.

He did what I asked: three pats after each pour.
"Pour, pat-pat-pat." Same on each side.

We won the prize for the tallest castle.
A berry slushy.

Straw Spoons

Back on our blankets,
he asks,

Want to try blueberry?
There's a spoon on the straw.

Oh.
Sure!

We watched the waves
wash over the castle.

I didn't need to try to save it,
like I would've before.

A straw spoon full
of blueberry slushy

tasted like friendship,
filled me with hope,

like how the beach
pours sky into my heart.

Naz

Naz gets to spend the night.
She brought her tape collection.

We talk and giggle like sisters,
even though we're not.

Some people assume we're related,
just because we're both Persian.

We belt out tunes to our pretend audience.
Perform a dance routine.
Bow.

Naz claps like it's real.
Her hair is thick with curls so tight,
her face is a flower of bouncing
dark brown petal springs.

She asks:

When are you going to get a perm?

Maybe in a few months.

I wish my hair was straight.

Oh my God! I wish my hair was curly!

Naz presses play on the boom box.
Our hair flies around as we sing and dance
to "Livin' on a Prayer."

Volunteering

You can be anything.

doctor
lawyer
or engineer

If you become a doctor,
you can always find a job.

While Maman rounds on patients,
the volunteer coordinator shows me
where to take mail,
how to deliver newspapers to patients,
how to push a wheelchair.

Every Saturday morning
from now through summer,

I'll have to be at the hospital
instead of at the beach,

instead of riding early with the surfers,
while Maman works
in labor and delivery.

Maybe you will be a doctor like me?

At the cafeteria,
I can drink all of the hot chocolate
I want,
but I'd rather have a slushy
at the beach.

Calls from Far Away

It's Baba.

Maman says
after she answers the phone.

She always sounds the same
when she is talking with him:
stiff, flat,
trying to forget
a song she once knew.

But I can hear the lyrics.

He says
my Naw-Rúz gift
is on its way.

I want to forget the way they talk,
how they have to figure it out.

My dresser is a mess.
Naz must have played with my earrings.
None of them are in the right spot.
I put each one in the right order.
The clock is turned a bit.
I straighten it.

I set my alarm.
Naz and I are meeting Phoenix
early tomorrow at the beach.

Seven a.m.
Seven a.m.
I check it one more time.
Seven a.m.

Ava? Maman's off the phone.
What are you doing?

Setting my alarm.
Did you move my clock?

No.

Your baba's
sending a gift to you,
for Naw-Rúz.

K.

I lis
present
is late,
as usual.

The Clock

I check the clock
one more time.

He
one more time
is
one more time
sending
one more time
a gift to me.

Check it,
check it,
check it,

because things
one more time
meant to stay
one more time
can
one more time

disappear.

Baba Means "Dad"

When someone asks about mine,
I say he lives far away.
He's in another country.
We visit sometimes.

But the words *baba* and *dad*
never feel
right.

I have one,
like half my DNA comes from him.
I have one,
like I got his skin color and thin frame.
I have one,
like my hair doesn't curl and frizz like Maman's.

But I don't have one,
like he has other kids now,
and my baby pictures
aren't in
his photo albums.

School Starts Tomorrow   Sunday, March 29

Today is the last day
of spring break.

Phoenix, Naz, and I
meet at the beach.
Seems like our whole
eighth grade
class is here.

I chew my Abba-Zaba.
The boardwalk booms
with shifting music
and shirtless skaters.

My skin tans into olive brown.
Naz sprays Sun In on her hair,
hoping it might turn blond.

Phoenix picks up his board.

Let's go already!

I grab
my board.
We run
toward the water.

We push through
the break.

We paddle
far out,

sit on bobbing boards,
watch the swells
boom ocean beats

        of forever.

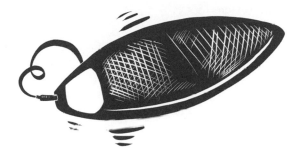

Getting Ready for School

I turn the radio on
right after I turn my alarm off.

I hear "Fight for Your Right."
I turn the volume up.

Like the moon pulls the waves,
the music lifts my breath
to sing and
makes it easy to forget,
it's just me
and Maman.

It turns my distant dad
into a sing-along
and getting ready for school
into a party
with the Beastie Boys.

Maman

fills her glass jam jar with hot tea.

Plastic makes it taste bad
and puts poison in the tea.

She balances the jar
between the parking brake and her car seat.

She'll drop me off at school
on her way to the operating room.

She made tea for me too,
and a sandwich of Wonder Bread
and feta cheese.

She carefully sips as she
drives onto the freeway on-ramp
that turns like the steam winding around her mouth.

I hold my glass cup with the glass handle,
watch the tea wave back and forth,
try to time when I can have a taste.

She delicately purses her lips
toward the caramel sugar and caffeine

that will get her through
the final suture of the day.

In medical school back in Iran,
she was one of a few
women.

In training back in New York,
she was one of a few
women.

In So Cal now,
she is one of a few
mother
doctor
surgeons.

Car Convo

Maman, can I
work at the Gap
this summer?

My baba said
education is freedom.

She takes a sip of tea.

This summer,
you don't need
to learn how to SELL clothes.

This summer,
learn some medicine.

Now is the time to study.
So you can always
get a job
make your own money
be able to BUY clothes.

She takes a sip of tea.

And always drink tea
from a glass cup.

The Sound of Honey Dripping

Maman's life is as opposite
to her mother's and her grandmother's
as sweet is to sour.

Her mother had fifteen babies.
Her grandmother married so young
it was more like an adoption
by another man's mother.

Maman has one kid,
is married to being a doctor,
has settled onto medicine
like honey on bāqlavā.

Though sometimes
the honey drips off
when she whispers
my father's name.

I wonder if she'd rather
be married to
a person instead.

Lunchtime Convo

We get up from the school lawn
where we kick back at lunch.

Naz says,

> *Hey Ava, wanna go*
> *to the mall Saturday?*
> *Maui and Sons*
> *has some rad new T-shirts!*

Oh man, remember?
I have to go
to the hospital
on Saturday.
Volunteer and get
"medical experience."

> *Oh yeah.*

You're so lucky
your parents are going to let you
get a job this summer,
while I'll be passing trays
to hospital patients.

> *Hospital food?*
> *Gag me with a spoon!*

When do you start
work at the snack shop?

> *Not for a few months.*

We get to our lockers
as Phoenix closes his.

Beach, when I'm done volunteering?

                                        I'm there! You too, Phoenix?

*The waves
should be cranking!*

He says:

                *Dude!
                Saturday, right?
                Where else
                would I be?*

Phoenix sets
his hand on my shoulder,
gives a shaka
with his other hand.

We head to fifth period
together,
past the lockers,
past the lawn,
like five years
haven't passed.

Outside-of-School Friends

Around third grade,
Phoenix and I
stopped hanging out much
at school.

Boys played handball.
Girls ruled the monkey bars.

Now, we're in different cliques.
He hangs with the surfers.
Naz and I sit with the preppies.

We're not
inside-of-school friends.

But Maman works
with Phoenix's dad,
a surgeon,
at the same hospital.

Phoenix's house
is behind mine.

Outside of school,
it's different.

We sit through family events
the hospital puts on,
hang out at neighborhood block parties.

His family even tries
to come to Maman's Persian
holiday celebrations,
even though the Skylers aren't Persian.

And mostly, we hang out
at the beach,
a few blocks away from home.

Outside of school,
Phoenix is like
a brother
I've never had.

Mondays and Wednesdays

are when choir meets
    after school.
    Ms. Rivers runs the group.

are my favorite days
    after Saturdays and summers.
    Naz is a soprano.

are when I'm an alto.
    Eighth graders
    get to stand in front.

are when Naz and I aren't
    Persian girls
    putting on a show.

We belt out tunes like
    Cyndi Lauper girls
    showing our true colors.

Lie of the Thirteen[3]

Pedaling home on our bikes,
we stop at the crosswalk.

Where you from? a stranger asks.

Here, I say.

Not with those curls. He laughs
and points at Naz's hair.

I was born in New York, I say,
hoping he'll shut up soon.

Ah! That makes sense.
You're Italian!

The light turns green.
We head home.
Naz shouts,

April fool!

For dinner, we eat spaghetti
and beef Bolognese
with turmeric and advīeh[4] spice.

After we eat, we watch TV.
Perfect Strangers is on tonight.

---

3. "Lie of the Thirteen" (Durūgh-i Sīzdah) is the Persian version of April Fools' Day. It is observed on the first or second day of April, the day of Sīzdah Bedar ("thirteen outdoors"), the thirteenth day of the Persian New Year. Pranks have been played on this holiday since 536 BC.

4. Advīeh is a Persian spice blend that is a staple in many Persian dishes. It is commonly made of a blend of cardamom, cumin, cinnamon, coriander, black pepper, turmeric, dried limes, cloves, and dried rose petals.

Party in the Park   Saturday morning, April 4

On Sīzdah Bedar,
thirteen days after Naw-Rúz
or, in America, the second Saturday after Naw-Rúz,
Persians picnic in the park.

I'm off volunteer duty today,
except volunteering to pretend
it's comfortable here.

Can't wait to get to the beach later.
Wore my swimsuit under
my shorts and T-shirt.

For this picnic you need:

> high heels
> big sunglasses
> a boom box
> backgammon
> cards

> Persian picnic food:
>> kūkū sabzī—spinach, greens, and egg patties
>> kutlit—ground meat, potato, and egg fritter
>> pickled garlic and fresh herbs
>> thick, creamy yogurt mixed with crunchy cucumber pieces
>> lavāsh bread and feta cheese
>> and a samovar of hot tea

> sprouts you grew for the Naw-Rúz Haft-Sīn.

Naz and I are supposed to
knot the sprout leaves
before tossing them into the lake,
> *Return it to nature.*
> *Block evil.*
while we
make a wish,
> *to find true love,*
to leave early.

Persian tracks

blare
from the outdoor dance floor.

We sit with Naz's family,
Persian rug as our picnic blanket.

Naz is rocking the tumbak[5]
with finger and palm slaps.

Maman is telling stories
of country picnics in Iran.

I play with the sprout leaves
like I'm tying a knot.

Look at Naz
while I nod toward the lake.

We make an escape,
throw green hope into the water.

My bunch of sprouts is
all unknotted.

The deep green blades remind me
of Phoenix's front door.

---

5. Persian goblet drum.

Front Door

When Maman dropped me off at Phoenix's
for his seventh birthday party,

the front door
had just been painted green.

The doormat said *welcome*.
Phoenix opened the door.

He said hello
like evergreen,

like we would always be
welcome to stay.

Cake

Even though Phoenix's birthday
was Monday, July 7,

his party was on a Saturday.
The whole first grade came.

Phoenix's mom made
a Rubik's Cube–themed cake.

Bel helped to decorate.
I didn't know

you could make cake
at home.

Phoenix Being Born

After all the kids left,
we were hanging in the living room.
Phoenix's mom told the story
of Phoenix being born.

> *Phoenix's dad had been*
> *up all night working*
> *while I was in early labor*
> *on another hospital floor.*
>
> *After getting some coffee*
> *from the cafeteria,*
> *he walked into a room,*
> *saw a baby in a bassinet.*
>
> *He went to pick the baby up.*
> *He thought he had missed it all.*
> *I could hear the mother scream!*
> *He walked into the wrong room!*
>
> *I didn't give birth for a few more hours,*
> *so he ended up not missing*
> *the delivery.*
> *Phoenix has his lips.*

Another Conversation

After the party,
we all walked to the beach
to watch the sunset.

Maman, what's the story
of the day I was born?
I remember, my dad wanted
to name me Nur.

　　　　　　　　　　　　It means "light."

　　　　　　　　　　　　I told your baba.
　　　　　　　　　　　　English speakers would have
　　　　　　　　　　　　a hard time saying it.

They used to have conversations,
about things besides
when to visit.

Who held me first?

Who did my baby lips
remind you of?

Maman drops in on my wave.

　　　　　　　　　　　　Your baba
　　　　　　　　　　　　wasn't there
　　　　　　　　　　　　the day you were born.

　　　　　　　　　　　　He was
　　　　　　　　　　　　in Paris.

But you were in New York?

We were.
But before you were born,
he went to Paris.

And he stayed there.

He wasn't around?
to see?
the birth?
of his baby?

Why didn't my dad stay in New York?

Why did Maman
let him leave?
Me being born
          wasn't enough
                    to feel like they belonged
                                        together,
                    to feel like I belonged
          to them.
Maman got to
name me Ava
without having

another conversation.

Two Kinds of Tears

That night,
as the sun set,
I learned

there are two kinds of tears.

When I was born, Maman cried

     happy tears,
          "happy to meet you" tears,

     and sad tears,
        goodbye tears,
        "we are alone" tears.

I learned,
if you love something
and don't want to lose it,
stay close to it.

Maman and my dad didn't
stay close to each other
and lost each other.

My dad didn't
stay close to me
and lost me.

The boom box
on the beach towel next to us
blasted "The Tide Is High,"
by Blondie.

I learned
why, sometimes,
people sing about
holding on
and not giving up.

Digging in the Sand

Phoenix and I
dug a huge hole
in the sand.

I tried to forget
what my dad wanted to
name me.

A wave came at us,

>   *Ava!*
>   Phoenix called.

My name was easy
for Phoenix to say.

He pulled my arm.
    We ran to dry sand,
        let the hole fill
            with water,
                with giggles
                    and shouts,
                with staying close,
            with happy tears
        and castles made
    of twilight
waves.

Ava

It's easy to pronounce.
It's a universal name,
Maman says.

From the Latin *avis*.

It means "bird."

Maybe she knew
we would escape a revolution,
that I wouldn't
grow up in Iran
and that I'd try to fly
past Persian expectations,
        patriarchal beliefs
        Mercedes Benzy
        Califarsi
        peach tract houses
        dressed like antique
        French villas.

From the Hebrew, of Eve,
it's a short form of *Chava*.

It means "life" or "living one."

Maybe she knew
I'd be the only one
to survive
her and my dad.

From the Persian *āvāz*,
"song."

It means "singing voice."

Maybe she knew
I'd have a voice
    in America,
      where I could speak
      or even sing
      and not be arrested
      for showing
      a little skin.

Beneath the Break   Saturday afternoon, April 4, 1987

Whirlucent blue
     salt waters my eyes,
          my mouth, my neck.
               Every brown lock
                    soaked
                              in turning
                                    curving tubes.
                              To ride is hope
                    in motion,
              trying to stay on.
        At least if I fall,
water bubbles
        tumble tumble
rumble beneath
     the break.
Hold my breath
     swim up to light
swim up to freedom.

46

Betty

I was a Barney until Phoenix
gave me surf lessons.

Now I'm a Betty.
I can pop up, trim, and pump.

Phoenix has been
shooting the curls for years,
can even backdoor into a barrel.

And even though for dinner tonight
I'll eat Persian rice and stew
and he'll eat chicken pot pie,

even though I sit with preppies
and he kicks it with surfers,

on our way back from the beach,
we walk home like we used to,

> before we knew about
> Barneys and Bettys,
> Izods and Vans,
> when we still played
> with sand buckets and shovels,
> while Maman and Phoenix's dad
> shared surgery stories.

*You got out
of the water
fast*, I say.

I'm not feeling it. Super tired.

I heard you playing guitar
at two a.m.

Maybe that's it.

We walk home like we used to,

share a candy bar
split a 7UP

until

he walks with me past
the front yard gate

all the way to
my front door

like he never used to.

Ms. Rivers is excited.   Monday, April 6

They've invited
students from our school
to perform at the Fourth of July
Freedom Festival!

You should do it.

But I've never been
onstage
by myself
before.

It's always been
with the choir.

After the parade,
during the picnic,
Ms. Rivers adds.

I'm sure
Maman wants me to
volunteer that day.

But it's a national holiday?

I'll think about it.

Contest Clothes

At home,
I try on
outfits,
see what could
work onstage.

I remember
what Maman said
about being able
to buy clothes.

But then the radio starts playing
"La Isla Bonita."

My bed becomes an island stage.
I'm dancing to the beat
in my old T-shirt

while my soul
is shredding in Armani

that can't be bought by money.

Isolation Rooms

My first job in the hospital
is to pass around the newspaper.

Not sure how this is
supposed to make me
like the idea of being a doctor.

Some hallways smell
like the mall bathroom
and there's no window to open.

After I place a few copies at the nurses' station,
a nurse tells me which rooms
I can walk into.

> *If a patient feels like*
> *talking with you,*
> *that's okay too.*
> *But knock first.*
> *Say you're a volunteer*
> *passing out the newspaper.*

Some doctors speak softly
outside of room 509.

> *That room is off limits though.*
> *That's an isolation room.*

I catch a glimpse of the patient
through the door window.

He's an older man.
Looks like he is blowing into a plastic toy,[6]
making a ball move up and down.

But it doesn't look like
he's having any fun.

Looks like he wants
some fresh air
as much as I do.

---

6. A lung exerciser that encourages deep breaths called an "incentive spirometer."

Alarm

It's time for bed.
Set the alarm
> *six thirty*
> *six thirty*
> *six thiiiiiirty*
> *six*
> *six*
> *six*
> *six*
> *six*
> *six . . . thirty*
> *Yes.*

Put the clock down.
Turn off the light.
> *Is it right?*
> *Is it right?*
> *Is it right?*

Turn the light on.
Set the alarm.
> *Six (is it?)*
> *Six (is it?)*
> *Six (is it?)*
> *Thirty (is it?)*
> *Thirty (is it?)*
> *Thirty (is it?)*

Okay, just one more time.
One more time.

Yes, it's six.
Yes, it's three.
Yes, it's zero.

> *six three zero six three zero*
> *six (STOP CHECKING!) six six*
> *six three zero (STOP!)*
> *six   three   (LOOK AWAY!)   zero.*

The numbers can't change.

What I see is what I see,
right?

But I still need to
check.

Don't Lose Another

Olive was my first pet.
Maman was afraid of dogs,
but a hamster was allowed.

She was soft, creamy tan colored.
She would get lost under
the brown fuzzy couch.

I was in charge of feeding her.
It wasn't hard.
Fill the water bottle, hang it back up.
Pour food into her food bin.

At least I could play
with her.
When she crawled on me,
it tickled.

But when you are the only one
looking out for something,
there's no backup,
no second chance,
no next time.

And I was her
only one.

Most of the time,
Maman was too tired to
remember to feed Olive.

One time, while I was sick,
I forgot to feed Olive.

And Maman forgot to feed Olive.

And Olive—

The vet said:

> *Keep a schedule,*
> *set an alarm,*
> *some kind of reminder,*
> *so you don't lose another*
> *Olive again.*
>
> *Don't forget*
> *to double-check.*

I have another hamster now.
Apricot.

I triple-check.

She's still
alive.

On the wall

in Ms. Rivers' room,
a new poster.

It's the Freedom Festival competition
she was telling me about.

I think I want to sign up,
but no one would want

to hear just me
sing.

Checking on Patients

Maman says,

> *Ava, I know you're done with*
> *volunteering for today.*
> *But I have to check on a patient*
> *before we go.*

Okay, I'll wait in the atrium.
After I get a hot chocolate.

> *Okay.*

Room 509 is also in the atrium.
I guess he's out of isolation.

He sits and watches the sky.

He starts talking
without looking at me.
> *Smoggy today,*
> *but still worth*
> *taking a breath*
> *and looking up.*

He looks over at me,
then back up at the sky.

You're not in
isolation anymore?

> *How'd you know I was in isolation?*

Oh, I volunteer here.
A nurse said to not go
into your room,
to give you a paper.

> *Oh, well now my immune system*
> *is back in shape,*
> *and I'm not in isolation anymore.*

Congratulations.

Was that the right thing to say?
Room 509 smiles anyway.

> *Thanks.*

I pull each side of my hoodie strings
until they are even.

He wheels himself to the door.

> *Next time you're on my floor,*
> *I'd love a paper.*

Sure.

In a Corner

Maman

      Guess what?

is excited.

      I asked one of my patients
      if you could stand
      in the corner of the room
      and watch her delivery.

Oh.
What?!

      I told her you
      and Claire
      would be quiet,
      out of the way.

Claire?

      Yeah, Claire is one of the
      other volunteers.
      She seemed excited to watch one.

But—

      It's such a great opportunity.

I'm kind of not—

      Think about it.

I have.

*Ava, don't you want to know
about my job?*

*You're already making me
volunteer at the hospital.*

*So many other kids would
love that chance.*

*I'm not
so many other
kids.*

*You could try to act
like a doctor's daughter?*

*You already don't act
like a Persian daughter.*

*So!
You don't act
like a Persian mom.*

Or an American one.

Maman's eyes become almond slivers
like every mom I've seen,
even American ones,
when they're angry.

While I Wait for My Dad to Call   Saturday night, April 18

My dad
is going to call.

He's late.

I should
remember
he's on
Persian time,
even though
he lives in Paris.

While I wait,
I listen to "Lean on Me"
on the mixtape Naz
made for me.

I straighten
the pillows of my bed.
Make sure the one
on the left
is the same distance
from the edge
as the one
on the right.

The song ends,
just as the phone
starts to ring.

                                        He can't
                                        see me

while we talk.

So, I fill Apricot's water bottle.
I look through
Surfer magazine.

I rewind the tape
until the counter reads 143
—the count where
"Lean on Me" starts.

So that when
the call is over, I   won't

have to   wait to
                                         hear my

new favorite   song,
I can just press   play.

Phoenix stops by.

Hey Ava.

Hey.

I have a present for you.

He hands me a new Walkman.
No way!
But these cost so much money?

So, it's not just from me.

What?

Your mom felt bad about
making you volunteer at the hospital.
She asked me and Naz
what might help.

Oh my God, and you said
A WALKMAN!

She asked me
to pick it out.

But it's from
"all of us."

His cheeks burn red.
Thank you.

This will totally help.

Gift

*So, there's something there
from me too.*

I look at the Walkman again
and see
that there's a tape inside.

I press eject
and pull the tape out.

It's a mixtape labeled
*For Ava, From Phoenix
Spring 1987*

This is awesome!

But he's already at
the gate.

You owe me!

I take the beanie hat off my head,
throw it as hard as I can at him.

*Nice.
Red's my favorite color.
He smirks.*

My cheeks burn.
You can keep it until . . .

Oh, it's mine now.

We'll s . . .

                                        . . . see you at school, Ava.

See ya, Phoenix.

I run inside.

Thank Maman
for the Walkman.

And then I listen to the
real gift.

Blood Draw

In my head, I call him "Room 509."
But his last name is Camden.
He's my last stop today
before I get to leave.
I knock on the door.

Hello? Room . . . I mean, Mr. Camden.
Can I come in?

                                    Yes.

A nurse stands next to his bed.
She draws 509's blood through a needle,
like it's found a hidden red river.
The vial fills with thick color.

                        Hey, no need to fuss
                        over your sweatshirt.
                        I can tell you're nervous.

                        This is just a routine blood draw,
                        making sure my immune system's
                        holding up.

I let go of my hoodie pulls.
Oh, I just like things even.

I put the newspaper on the bedside tray.

                        Like the two piles of paper
                        on your cart?

I try to keep them the same height.

I guess.

Do the blood draws scare you?

> *Not anymore.*
> *But if I get worked up,*
> *I take some deep breaths.*
> *That usually calms me down.*

Oh.

Maybe for me,
keeping things even
kind of feels like deep breaths.

The nurse pulls the needle out.
She tapes a cotton ball to Room 509's arm.
509 reaches over, with the cotton ball arm,
to pick the newspaper up off the tray.

> *Hey,*

He squints at my volunteer badge.

> *Ava.*
> *Thanks for remembering*
> *to bring a paper by.*

Sure.
See you
next week.

Beneath Skin

I walk
out of the room
with the nurse.

I stop to straighten my
hoodie pulls.

The nurse
pushes a cart
carrying
vials of crimson.

I feel off-balance.
I grab the handrail in the hall.

Everything is spinning.

All I can see is that color
                    of sunset fire,
                            rolling lava,
                                    and red plums,
                                            beneath his skin,
                                    and the next patient's,
                            it's also
                    under
        mine.
Thump.

Out Early

The nurse
waves something
in front of my nose.

I'm flat on the floor,
looking at the ceiling.

Can you hear me? she shouts.

I nod.

She's okay.
She just fainted.

The volunteer coordinator
sends me home early.

Get some rest, Ava.

Each Exhale

That night, I dream.

Phoenix

is drowning
in a bloodred ocean.

The ocean waves are made of millions of spears.
The spears pierce green monsters that rise out of the red water.

Evil clouds explode from the monsters, then vanish,
every time a wave of spears breaks onto the monsters.

After the last monster is hit,
Phoenix surfs under a clear starlit sky.
He drops into a glowing red wave tube.

Starting at Phoenix's body and moving outward,
the ocean turns every color of blue.
The tube turns into a whirlpool.

Phoenix drops into the dark center
right as the ocean becomes his blue eyes.

He lays on his beach blanket,
breathes so deeply,
each exhale

lights the sunrise.

Choir Class

Altos don't usually
get the melody.

But today, Ms. Rivers asked
for altos to solo
in one of the school's
spring concert songs.

My hands are a soaked sponge
someone starts to squeeze.

From under my arms,
drops roll down my side.

My cheeks turn into August
midafternoon boardwalk cement.

I step forward for my part.

The words echo off the walls.

I have to close my eyes,
like when you jump
from just too high.

I've sung alone for crowds
in my room
and audiences
in my head.

Now, it's for class,
Ms. Rivers,
and soon the school.

After the first line,

        I forget my body.
                I forget the dread.
                        I forget the sweat. I forget
                              who I have been and who left.
                        I only feel now o'clock.
                Each note's a stitch.
        I'm a cut, getting mended.

After Class

I point to the competition poster on the wall.

I can sing a song someone else has sung before.

Ms. Rivers,
you can
>*sign*
>*me*
>*up.*

Run up to Our Spot

Bag down.
Towel out.

Cheh khabar?
Phoenix shouts
as he walks up.

He's known
that phrase
since we were little.
It's the Persian "What's up?"

Hameh chīz khūbeh.[7]

I'm done with volunteering today.
I passed out
mac and cheese in the cafeteria.

Nice. Not ham and cheese?

Remember. . . when I thought . . .
hameh chīz
was . . .

He's cracking up.

"ham and cheese"?

---

7. *Hameh chīz khūbeh* means "everything's good" in Farsi.

That was totally . . .

I was waiting
for a ham-and-cheese sandwich . . .

for like an hour
after you heard that
at the first Persian party
you came to!

We laugh so hard,
we can barely
breathe.

After we catch
our breath,

Cheh khabar with you?

Think I'm getting
over a cold.

At least the water's
glassy today.

Yeah.
Let's go!

Kick Out

On our boards,
as we watch the swells,

I sing "Lean on Me."

Sounds good, Phoenix says.

*Thanks, I'm going to sing it
at the Freedom Festival competition.*

Ms. Rivers said I should sign up.

Cool.

*Hey, when is the choir concert?
I want to go.*

*Since when do surfers
come to choir concerts?*

*Since their friends have to go
to their guitar recitals.*

*Next Saturday morning.
Remember, you owe me.*

He winks.

*Oh man.
I have to volunteer that morning.*

Your mom will totally let you.
I'll tell Bel to save you
a seat.

This wave's mine!

Phoenix paddles hard,
floats on the lip,
rides onto the face,
finishes with a kick out.

But instead of heading back to the line,
he heads to the white water,
the way he does when he's had
enough surf for the day.

Leaving me alone
on the outside,
earlier than I thought
he would.

Chillin' on Our Towels

Some guys our age
are playing volleyball nearby.

Their ball rolls to our spot.
One of them runs over to pick it up.

Hey. What language was that?

When we were laughing earlier,
he must have
heard us and wondered
what was up.

Phoenix says,
                    Farsi

What?

I say, *Persian*

What's that?

*What people speak
in Iran, dude.*

*That place that took hostages
for more than a year?!*

Volleyball guy
looks at me,
then Phoenix.

His face looks like
he just got stung
by a jellyfish.

Phoenix says,

> *Some wack people did that,*
> *man.*
> *Not a place.*
> *Persians and Farsi*
> *have been around*
> *for thousands of years.*

> *Oh really.*
> *Maybe not much longer though?*
> *Huh?!*

Volleyball guy looks at me.
He launches hate from his eyes.

Phoenix throws the ball back to him,
making the guy run after it,
because it passes
over his head.

Stare at the Sun

Maman lets me leave the hospital early
to see Phoenix's recital.

I sit next to Bel and her parents.
I've never seen Phoenix onstage before.
He's been taking guitar lessons for a few years.

He starts to play: "Here Comes the Sun."

He closes his eyes,
like I did when I sang my solo at choir practice.

His song is like a window,
      but I have to close my eyes
           to look through it, then I see what can
               burn me blind but lights the world up.

Bel and his parents see it too,
        their faces glow, like when he was nine
           and they told me and Maman
               Phoenix's lymphoma cancer was finally gone.

It feels like I can stare at the sun
        when it shines through a song,
           when it rides on guitar string waves
               made by his hand as it strums.

After Choir Practice   Wednesday, May 20

We were all a little nervous during class.
The choir recital is next week.

I pack my backpack:
binder, pencil case, wallet, keys
binder, pencil case, wallet, keys
binder, pencil case, wallet, keys

You okay, Ava? Ms. Rivers asks.

Oh, yeah umm
Make something up, Ava!
I think I   may have lost something.

What is it?

My hospital ID.

Oh, are you volunteering there?

Yeah.

That's special.
Where your mom works?

Mm-hmm.

Well, I hope you find it.

Thanks.

binder, pencil case, wallet, keys
I know,

binder, pencil case, wallet, keys,
exactly where my badge is.

binder, pencil case, wallet, keys
I haven't lost it. But maybe

I should.

Labor

Ava, today you get to see
a baby being born.

I *GET TO?*

When other kids went to work with their parents,
this is *not* the kind of stuff they did.

Maman takes me around the L and D[8] ward.
She's dripping with pride.

This is my daughter, Ava.

Most of the staff already know me,
pick up my calls
when the sitter needs Maman's permission
to let me watch more TV.

Sometimes I sit at the nurses' station
while Maman rounds.

Maman shows the call room to me,
where the doctors *might* rest,
when they work for thirty-six hours straight.

It's small and dark.
There's a twin bed,
a bedside table with a phone on it,
a paper box of rough tissues,
and a small lamp.
The walls are bare.

---

8. Short for Labor and Delivery, the area of the hospital where mothers have their babies.

I change into hospital scrubs,
put on blue paper shoe covers
and a thin head cap.

As I walk by the nurses' station,
a nurse hands a mask to me.

I put it on over my nose and mouth.
Wish I hadn't had eggs for breakfast.

Delivery

The baby's father is in the room.
A camera sits on the bedside table.

I stand with Claire,
near the door,
but we can still see.

She says,

I'm so excited to get to see this!

*My dad fainted when I was born.
How about yours?*

I answer,
Mine? I don't . . . he . . .

The nurse counts.

*Push! 1, 2, 3, 4, 5, 6, 7, 8, 9, 10!
Breathe out then in
then push! 1, 2, 3, 4, 5, 6, 7, 8, 9, 10!
Breathe out then in
then push! 1, 2, 3, 4, 5, 6, 7, 8, 9, 10!*

The nurse stands on one side of the bed,
next to the mother's shoulder.

The father stands
at the other shoulder.

And push, 1, 2, 3, 4, 5, 6, 7, 8, 9, 10!

They

breathe, push, count
breathe, push, count
breathe, push, count
breathe

A bulge of hair.
A head.
Then a body
slips
out.

> It's
> a
> girl!

The mother smiles wide
and cries.

The father kisses her forehead
and cries.

As we leave the room,
Claire beams.

> Congratulations!
> Thank you for letting us be here!

I follow with,
Thank you.

Complications

But my eyes
are also soaked
'cause
my mind's racing with visions:

first meetings,
a mom, a dad, and their baby,
first *hellos*.

That scene
fights against

no meeting,
when there is no dad
to stand
to count
to say hi
to cry

when I was born.

Wasn't I
worth it?

Didn't he
want to
say hi
when I
arrived?

Backstage

I can't get the image of baby girls
coming into the world
out of my head.

Are some welcomed,
and some not?

But I need to focus
on my voice,
on the choir recital
tonight.

Behind the curtains:
makeup, black skirts,
green-striped tops.

Step on the risers
quietly.

Ms. Rivers tells the crowd:

Find your chairs.
We're about to
start.

Through the curtain seam

a line of light,

then

the theater goes dark,
        audience chatter
                becomes a murmur
                        becomes a hush

here it comes,
        the spotlight
                lands on us,
                        we're all that matters

we're the new baby
        crying, as our lungs
                inhale the sky
                        and open up.

My Choir Solo

I hear my voice,

    really hear it;

        it's a newborn blanket

           wrapping around my

               shaking arms and legs.

                  I'm calm in the swaddle,

                     held up by   the stage

                                    the crowd
                                    cheers

                                    a tidal wave of

                                    hellos.

Memorial Day Weekend Saturday, May 30

Don't have to volunteer
at the hospital today.

Naz and I meet
at the pier to hang out
before her shift.

The overcast mist
of So Cal June gloom
is so thick,

even my straight hair
is frizzing.

Off

So glad I'm off today.
The recital was rad, right?

Yeah. Totally.
You made it through the solo—
we all knew you would.

Thanks, Naz.

Come visit the snack shop
during my shift.

Only if you save
an Abba-Zaba for me.

Just one?

Ha. I wish you
worked at the hospital too,
instead of the new girl.

Is she cool?

Kind of.
It's annoying how
she's so into
volunteering.

We walk farther out

on the pier,
where we used to practice
cartwheels, spin above
crackling water.

What're you doing?

I dig though my backpack.
Looking for my badge.

Your hospital badge?

Here it is.

What do you need it for?

*I don't
need it for
anything
ever.*

We reach

the end of the pier.

As hard as
I can,
I throw the badge

over
the
edge.

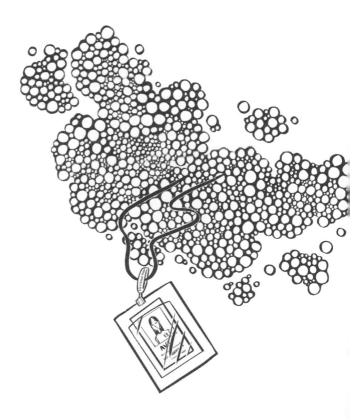

Out Loud

Naz shouts.

Ava, what'd you do?!

Words I've never said out loud
but have always turned in me
swell up and out.

*That badge is why
I don't have a dad, why
I don't have a sister or a brother.*

*It's the only thing Maman thinks
I should be.*

*Ava, you,
you have me.
We're like sisters.*

It's not the same.

*Okay, I know.
But maybe that
badge isn't
so bad?*

*C'mon, Naz.
As if!*

*Man, you always
have been the good little
Persian girl.*

What's that supposed to mean?

You know.
You play the tumbak
and like to pass out tea.

You act just like
the Gucci-wearing ladies,
follow all the rules.

                                        Ava, don't . . .

Don't you?
Like a good Persian daughter,
kissing up to the other moms.

Like Sisters

Ava, remember how you
felt onstage last night?

I shut up.

That's what I feel
when I play tumbak.

And that badge,

maybe that badge
makes your Maman feel
the same way.

Naz walks away.

I hear the words,
I just said
out loud
for the first time,

pounding
through the air,
over and over again.

From My Towel

I can see
Naz working
at the snack shop.

I put on my headphones.

I check
on the Walkman
in my backpack
to make sure it's
        cool and covered.

So the tape
        won't warp.

I press play.
        The music
                pulses
                        with the
                                waves,
                        the surfers,
                and Phoenix,
        out in bright
green corduroy.

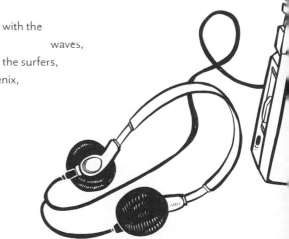

On Phoenix's drop

another rider cuts in.

Phoenix falls
and slams the water hard.

I don't see him
come up.
He isn't up.
He isn't up.

I rush
toward the water.

Phoenix!

The lifeguard
and I dive in.

We reach the board
right as Phoenix

surfaces.

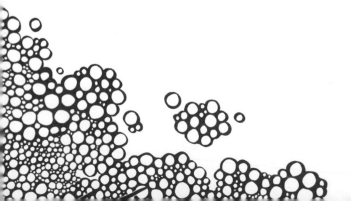

Phoenix, are you okay?!

Phoenix coughs and spits
as he hangs on
to the rescue buoy.

The lifeguard pulls him
to the sand.

What happened?

A snake cut you off!

Huh?

On the edge

of the water,
we lay
and catch our breath.

Do you
remember
falling in?

                I remember
                popping up
                then waking up
                underwater.

Waking up?
Maybe we should
check in with your dad?

                No, Ava, I'm fine.
                I just lost my grip.

Do you remember falling in?

                You need to chill.

Chill?!
I'm just trying to help.

                If you want to help,
                just get me a drink.

If you're fine,
you can get
your own drink.

Caught Inside

Naz looks worried
as I walk up.
Two 7UPs please.

                                    It's a dollar.
                                    Is Phoenix okay?

I don't know.
He doesn't remember
what happened.

                                    Freaky.

Naz hands me
two cold 7UP cans.

Thanks.
I feel bad about
what I said to Naz.

This one's for Phoenix.
And what I said to Phoenix.

I leave one can at the register.

He'll get it himself.
I'm heading home.

Naz reaches her hand out toward me.
I take the Abba-Zaba.

                                    You coming to the party tonight?

Like I have a choice?

Fights

with friends
make alone
feel like
empty.

Mihmūnī at Naz's

We're right on time,
nine p.m.
for dinner.

Little girls run around in silk dresses.
Boys are in button-down shirts and ties.
All the adults dress to impress.
The older kids and teens wear their labels:
Guess, Esprit, J.Crew, Benetton.

I wear the Benetton sweater,
because Naz gave it to me
for my birthday last September,
with my nice jeans
and my new slip-on Vans.

I go straight to Naz's room.
Music from her room
gets louder as I near her door.
Her tumbak sits next to the door.

Until now, I've never noticed
the ridges carved all around it,
like waves of water,
when it looks like corduroy.

Pretty gnarly she can
play the tumbak.

I knock,
harder and harder.

She finally opens the door.
I'm
sorry,
Naz.

What you said
was
totally rude.

I know.
I was mad about
Maman making me
volunteer.

And me being so Persian.

I was wrong, Naz.
I'm sorry.

No duh!

She's still mad at me.

But then,
she notices my sweater.

She gives me a hug
while she asks,

You tell your mom
about the badge yet?

No way.

But it won't
make a difference.
They'll just give me
a sticker to wear
while they make
a new badge.

"With or Without You"
starts playing from the boom box.

We sit on her bed,
listen to Bono and sing
the lyrics.

But it felt so good
to let the water

carry that badge
away.

Greetings

Naz's mom calls us
downstairs.

Enter a Persian party
and you're greeting

every.
single.
person.
there.

Her parents,
her mom's five brothers and sisters,
her dad's six brothers and sisters,
her grandparents, the two that got out of Iran in time,
her twenty cousins,
and a bunch of people you don't recognize,
but they know your name
and are surprised by how much
you've grown.

Handshake
and a kiss
on both cheeks.

When you're done,
your face has been dunked
in Armani cologne and
Chanel Eau de Parfum.

Mrs. Saks Fifth Avenue squeals,

Ava!
I found something!
I stepped on top of it
while I take my walk
on beach today.

She sifts through
her Yves St. Laurent.
She pulls out a plastic bag
with my badge inside.

Everyone Is a Jūn[9]

> *Ava jūn,*
> *what happened?*

Maman heard the squeal.

> *Oh, I must have lost this*
> *while I was at the beach.*

> *It looks like you can still use it*
> *until the hospital*
> *makes a replacement.*

Mrs. Saks squeals again,

> *You can still become doctor,*
> *Ava jūn!*

Naz's dad shouts,
> *Let's get them through junior high first!*
He cracks open
pistachios.
He chews heartily on the nuts
as he cheers,
> *Graduation is next week!*

Mrs. Saks chews on a date,

> *Māshālāh![10]*
> *Naz jūn,*
> *let's have some tea!*

---

9. In Farsi, *jūn* means "life." When said after someone's name, it means "dear."
10. In Arabic, *māshālāh* means "God has willed it." Said in many languages and cultures, such as the Persian culture, to also express congratulations, praise, and gratitude.

Tumbak

After dinner,
Naz breaks out the tumbak.

She can keep a beat like
the roller skaters cruising
on Ocean Drive.

Mrs. Saks can't
help but dance

in the middle of the room
as the rest of the party claps.

Naz's fingers, knuckles,
palms, and wrists

snap, click, slam
the drum suede.

Her hands
know how to sing.

My best girlfriend
is rockin' this Persian
show-off parade.

Car rides home

with Maman,
are often where I
get news about my dad.

He'll be able to
come to my
graduation.

They won't
sit near each other.

But we can take
some pictures
together.

What's the use
of me having pictures
of them, with me,
when that's not how
when that's not we
when that's not how we
live?

Last Choir Class

I'm sad I won't
ever have Ms. Rivers
as a teacher again.

At the end of class,
as we're packing up our stuff,
she puts the flyer
about the Freedom Festival competition
on my desk.

I'll see you at this?

I've been working on "Lean on Me."
But I'm not sure I'm
ready
to be alone onstage.
It's not perfect yet.

You're going for perfect?

Yeah. I want it to be good.

Connect
with the people listening.
If you do, it'll be
better than perfect,
'cause it'll be
true.

Wrap the Words

How do I connect? I ask.

Ms. Rivers' hazel eyes
stay stuck on my eyes
as she answers.

Remember what the lyrics mean:
friends leaning on each other.

Wrap that hope,
your heart,
around the words,
around the notes.

That's when a singer

She says like she's onstage.

and a listener

I watch like an audience.

connect.

Graduation Day

We arrive before
my dad.

He actually arrives
on time.

Maman nods her head,
fake smiles when she sees him.

I walk over.
My dad and I hug,
kiss on each cheek.

                                        Congratulations.

Thanks.

He finds
a seat
in the back.

Tension

When you have to
be with people
that don't want to be
together,

they're only there for
you

reminders of
mistakes,
walking away,
separate lives.

What is gone
still somehow
stays
in you.

Behind Me

Phoenix's family:

  Bel waves to me. Next year, she'll be the one graduating.

Naz's parents:

  Her dad rests their new VHS video recorder
  camera on his shoulder.

Maman:

  Her face is thick with makeup she doesn't usually wear.

My dad:

  On the other side of
  the auditorium.

A Few Rows Ahead

Naz's graduation cap
is studded with bobby pins
grasping her thick curls.

Phoenix's cap
is crooked;
he doesn't care.

     He turns around,
     waves to his family.

     He looks at me,
     his forehead wrinkled,
     eyes wide,
     tongue sticking out to one side.

     Then he raises a can of 7UP
          he snuck in with his smirk.
               My heart pops up on the crest of a wave.

     I look ahead to what's in front.
          I'm ready to drop. And leave
               Maman and my dad's separation behind.

Split

After the ceremony,

we're all taking pictures,
         before the party
         getting set up
         in the gym.

Naz's mom takes a picture of
         me with Maman,
         me with my dad,
         me between them.

At my back,
         Maman's hand on my lower waist,
         my dad's on my shoulders.
         In between:

                  My body separates
                  at the chest,
                  my heart

                  split.

Mend

Until I see
Phoenix's face,
goofy again.

Naz and I laugh.

We three
walk away
toward the gym.

My heart
gets bound
back together,
by friends.

Graduation Party

DJ
Doritos
strobe lights
signing yearbooks

Phoenix walks up.

I got my own 7UP.

I saw.

*Thanks for making me laugh
during the pictures.*

That looked super awkward.

It was like sooo . . .

I know.

*How're you doing since
the fall?*

I'm okay.

*Look,
I feel bad about . . .*

*Yeah, that was
kinda low.*

I was just trying to help.

Yeah. I know.
I'm sorry.

Listen, I'm going
to take off
early tonight.

But the party's just starting?

You know, I'm not
big into dancing.

Yeah.

Will . . .
Naz pulls my arm
toward the dance floor.

I'll see you at the beach.
Phoenix waves.

Tomorrow?

So many people are
jumping and dancing
in between us,
next time I look
where he was standing,
he's gone.

Dance

In the crowd

get away

feel nothing else

but what is

of me

for me.

Let the beat drown

any aches:

a distant dad,

separated parents,

wishing Phoenix didn't leave,

that he liked to dance.

Does his heart also

ride the crest of a wave

when I smile?

Pray with jumps and shouts

that this feeling lasts.

Speakers blast

Run-DMC's

"It's Tricky."

First Day of Summer, at the Hospital

My hospital badge
is warped,
with some sand stuck to it.

I like it so much more.
A piece of the ocean is with me
in the place that feels farthest from it.

I leave my visit to Room 509
to the last
of the day.

I hand him the newspaper.

> *Thanks.*
> *What's new?*

I graduated from eighth grade last night.

> *Oh.*
> *Congratulations.*
> *I bet your parents*
> *were proud.*

Yeah.
But, um, they're divorced.

> *What does that have to do*
> *with being proud*
> *of their daughter?*

Well, it was kind of
awkward.

I see. For you or for them?

For all of us!

Listen, I don't expect
you to understand,
anyone, to understand,
except Phoenix.

So, let's just talk about
something else.

You . . . have any good plans
for the summer?

Hangin' at the beach,
surfing
with Phoenix.

Singing songs
to the radio.

Nice. I miss seeing
the ocean.

And drinking those
blueberry slushies.

First Day of Summer, at the Beach

I haven't seen
Phoenix yet.

A little peeved
he left early
last night.

So I head in
alone.

Catching Waves

Paddle toward the edge of the world.

Catch a wave.

> Like clouds are billowing
> > beneath and I am the eagle
> > > that the storm can't hold.

Catch a wave.

> Hold gravity's hand
> > like a falling comet
> > > that just touched the stars.

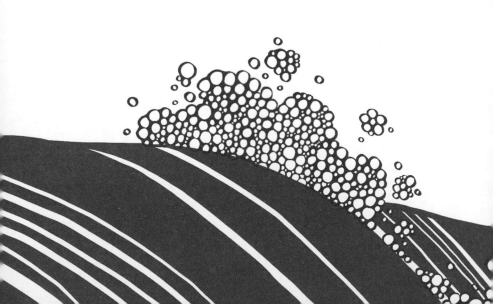

Release

That breath just after
I get knocked under,
then surface,
releases
the pain that throbs in my veins.

Phoenix ditching our graduation party,
olive skin that's not from here,
the weight of eyes
watching how I pass tea
or if my skirt's too high
or Maman's too free.

The water
takes the hurt
and pounds
it into the sand.

The water
gives me back
its pulse

unbound.

Hints

He walks
toward the water,

off-balance,
like he has a cramp.

He duck dives
toward me.

We meet
in the lineup.

Hey.

Hey, how was the party?

It was good.

I was mad you left,
but now that I've
caught some waves
and you're here,
I don't care anymore.

Especially the DJ.

Schweet!

You okay?

Looked like you
had a cramp while
you were walking over.

Yeah, paddling out helped.

Cool.

What would really help is
a new lighter board.

Ha!

Never too early
for birthday gift hints.

Where am I going
to get the money
for a gift like that?

The Freedom Festival competition.

Like I'm going to win that.

Duh, you are.

Even if I do,
I'm spending the prize money
on tapes.

Nice.

Well, if my parents
get me a new board
or tapes,
I'll share them with you.

Guess I'm a better friend
than you are.

He smirks.
I smirk back,
'cause I know.

Bel, his parents, and I
already have
hidden the new board
in their attic.

Go Back

You put something on my towel?

                                    No.

We get closer
to our stuff.

My sunscreen bottle
is covered in sand.

The cap is open
with sunscreen spilling out of it,

connected to words
written on my towel

in sunscreen.

*GO HOME
TERRORIST!*

                                    Here.

Phoenix hands me his towel
so I can dry off.

He rolls mine up
into his pack.

June

Sleep in like
morning starts at eleven a.m.

Write out lyrics like
there'll be a test on them.

Ride the Cali sea like
I was born here.
'Cause I was.

Sing in my room like
everyone's hanging
on my words.

Music on so loud,
I can't hear anything else.

Music on so loud,
I don't hear how *different* sounds.

June gloom mornings,
cold gray clouds.
My dad not around.
Maman's pressing
me into a medical nerd.
So Cal saying
I'm too brown.

After noon,
they all burn
into blue skies
over a beach that gives me
waves
no matter what.

Distracted

Saturday morning, June 27

Brought my favorite mixtape,
the one Phoenix made.

Wear my Walkman,
while I fill
the delivery cart with
newspapers, mail, flowers.

Oh, this song.

I haven't written
the lyrics out yet.

I grab a pen.

Listen, write, rewind,
        check the words,
                these verses,
                        like unwrapping a candy bar,
                this chorus like
        a bite into the nougat,
sugar bathes my heart.

Too Late

When it's all written down,
I push the cart out
of the mail room
to the elevator.

Doors open
and there she is,
the volunteer coordinator.

You're late.
You better get moving
or your mom's going to
hear about it.

I'll still be done by noon.

Plan on finishing even earlier
to show her.

Run between the patient rooms.

Don't see
the yellow warning sign
until
it's too late.

Hospital Floors

slip up

          trip

land hard

          ankle twists

pull

          pop

shooting pain

          my foot won't hold

me up

          wheelchair

                    X-ray

Don't

Don't take away my summer

don't take away dancing in my room
don't take away singing as I stand on my bed
don't take away my chance on a stage
don't take away my rides in the waves
don't take away my time with Naz
don't take away my time with Phoenix
don't take away our last summer

before ninth grade.

Fractured

Avulsion fracture.

*A piece of bone cracked off
by a muscle's pull,*
the doctor says.

*Six weeks.
Don't get the cast wet.
Surfing's out.*

My summer, shattered.

Trash Bags   Saturday afternoon, June 27

Maman brings home a box
of plastic trash bags.

I can wear them around my cast.
Still go to the beach.
Sit on a towel at least.

I want to throw the box
into the wall.
It's her hospital that made me fall,
broke my summer.

I hold my anger in,
don't let the swell rise,
but it's weak,
doesn't even bubble over.

I take the box.
Say thanks.
Tears soak my cheeks
as I walk to my room.

I'm sorry, Ava.

I know.

I blast "Shattered Dreams"
from the boom box.

I throw the box of trash bags
into the wall.

Me sitting at the beach
with a trash bag on my leg
is not what this summer was
supposed to be.

Help

Naz comes over.

She carries our stuff
across the sand.

We try to
have a

beach day.

I lay back and
listen to the
sky.

I stare at the
waves

crash.

Notes

Naz asks,

> Is your ankle hurting too much?
> Want to head back?

No, it'll hurt more at home.

> Hey, want to try "Lean on Me"?

Here?

> Yeah, why not?
> The competition is going to be
> right there at the pier.
> Pretend it's the Fourth.
> I'm the crowd.

I'm not sure I . . .

> I think you can.
> It'll take your mind
> off of your ankle.

I start to sing it, soft 'cause
I'm the one doing the leaning.

On the second verse,
Naz harmonizes with me.

We close our eyes,
sway to the sound
of how notes can
hold each other.

And even though I'm not
riding on the waves,
the song's like water,
and on it, I float.

A New Class

Maman signed me up
for a medicine for teens class
since I won't
be able to
do much as a volunteer now.

Every Monday and Wednesday.

Claire is in it too.

All I can think about is
how I hate the hospital.
And how I still need
to prep for the competition
on the Fourth.

Claire is taking
notes
as soon as
the teacher starts.

The class is going to begin
with learning about
vital signs and CPR,
cardio-pulmonary resuscitation.

Blah blah

Vital Signs

Respiratory rate:
>number of breaths a minute
>watch the chest go up and down
>listen to the air move

Pulse:
>number of heartbeats a minute
>check it—carotid, radial, femoral

Blood pressure:
>the power of heartbeats,
>pumping blood up to the head
>and down to the toes,
>faint if it's too low

CPR

Call 911.

Blow air into the patient's mouth,
          like wind behind the wave.

Keep the heart pumping
with hands pressing
on the chest,
          like when I pump my surfboard
          to keep the ride going
          a little longer.

Count it out.
Practice on a mannequin.

Keep the time
          like a song,
          like the Bee Gees'
          "Stayin' Alive."

New Job

After class,
I learn that
the volunteer office
has found a new job for me:
reading to patients.

One of them
is Room 509.

Time

Phoenix's parents invite
me and Maman
over for dinner.

Bel walks out of her room.
She's smiling.

Here, Ava.

She hands me
her guitar.

*I got a new one and
want to give you my old one.*

We'll teach you some chords.

*It'll give you something to do
while your ankle heals.*

*That is so rad!
Thank you, Bel.*

Also rad,
the time
she just gave me back,
with Phoenix.

A Major

I hold Bel's old guitar.

Its body,
under my right arm,
presses against me
like the back of my board
when I carry it.

The guitar neck fits
in my left hand.

High E
slices into my finger
when I press on it,
like a fin cutting water.

Phoenix and Bel show me
A major.
It looks like a wave,
I can ride with a strum.

A Dose

Some patients want me to read
the paper to them.
Some, letters from family.
Some, short stories or novels.

Room 509 asks for poetry.

He hands me
a three-ringed binder full of poems.
He collects poems in the binder.

One of the divider tabs is labeled
"Rumi."

Maman likes Hāfiz more.

You know Rumi?

*Well, my parents grew up in Iran,
so we have books by both.*

*Would you please read
one of the Rumi poems?*

*A Persian friend
translated them for me,
into English.*

Sure.

509 closes his eyes.

All day and night, music,
a quiet, bright
reedsong. If it
fades, we fade.[iii] —Rumi

When I am done,
his eyes stay closed.

He seems to be
somewhere else.

Are you okay?
Should I call the doctor?
Are you in pain?

                              Not anymore.

Has it been a while since
you've had your medications?

                    I had them this morning.
                    But those words, in the poems,
                    they're my second dose.

Performing on July Fourth

It's my first time onstage

alone.

I hobble on.

My fingers tingle.
My heart swells into my ribs.

Lights shine into my eyes,
so bright, I can see only
the mic and a few people
who stand leaning
on the stage.

Maman, Naz, and Phoenix are
in the front row.

Then everything is silent,
except the music from the speakers.

I hear my voice through the mic.
Every note loud and important.

Before,
I wasn't sure,

if I could get through the performance,
if I'd remember the words,
if I'd let myself be myself onstage,
with everyone staring at me.

Would they question whether
I deserved to stand up here?

Would *I* question whether
I deserved to stand up here?

But I hear myself now,
and the answer is

not anymore.

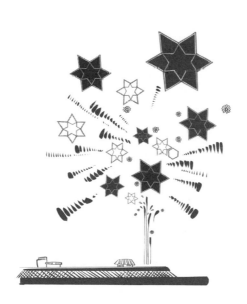

I sing

someone else's words but

right now they are mine.

We blast through clouds

into the clear black.

My heart   explodes

into thousands of

glimmering sparks.

Time doesn't matter.

Place doesn't matter.

All that's left

is the

glow.

Maman Sees It

She's tapping her hand on her thigh.
Closes her eyes
while she smiles.

❋ ❋ ❋

Naz Sees It

She's singing along with me.
Her mouth moving like a melody
I can hear
with my eyes.

❋ ❋ ❋

Phoenix Sees It

He's nodding his head to the rhythm.
He cheers like a drumbeat
I can feel
in my bones.

Ms. Rivers Sees It

She announces first prize.

       Perform at the Thanksgiving Concert on the Pier.
       Private lessons with Ms. Rivers.
       And one hundred dollars cash.

       The rest of us will get gift certificates
       to the Wherehouse.

I see her lips moving
but stop hearing her words.

She moves her hand
toward me
with the envelope.

First prize.

We hug
until—

I See It

Every smile and prize,
every melody and beat,
sucked into a gasp.

Two Breaths

A crowd in a circle.
Phoenix lies on the ground.

His dad beats *staying alive*
on Phoenix's chest.

I run over.
I fall on my knees
by his side.
His dad shouts.

Ava! Quick! Give two breaths!

hhhhhhhhhhaaaaaaaa
whhhhhhhhhhhhooooooooooo

hhhhhhhhhhaaaaaaaa
whhhhhhhhhhhhooooooooooo

Lifeguards

take over,
feel a pulse.

EMTs arrive.
They roll Phoenix onto the board.
Lift him to the gurney.
Slide him into the ambulance.

Phoenix's dad
steps up beside him.

His dad's lips move
while he holds Phoenix's hand.

I move
in closer
until an EMT
tugs me back
by the shoulder,

then
shuts the doors.

I run

like my pounding feet might open
the ambulance doors.

But my cast is too heavy.
My ankle feels like it's on fire.

The red lights
get farther
with each step.

Ava!
Naz screams.

HOOOONK!
A truck swerves around us.

Naz pulls me
from the intersection.

I fall onto the sidewalk.

Maman runs up.

Cheh ghalati daari mikoni![11]

she shouts.

Phoenix!

Ava, enough. You will get hurt!
We should go home
and wait by the phone.

---

11. Farsi for "What the heck are you doing?"

I stumble under
my weight.
I ran without
my crutches.

Maman and Naz
hold me up
on either side
as I limp back.

Ms. Rivers is still
on the stage
holding my crutches
with one hand,
the prize envelope
in her other hand.

Her eyes give me a hug,
then she looks at Maman.

I know you all don't live far,
but let me give you a ride.

At Home

I pick up the phone
I pick up the phone
I pick up the phone

every minute
to make sure
I hear a dial tone.

Ava,
he had a pulse
when they left.
He'll be okay,

Maman says.

But I can hear her say
Khudā as she chants
a prayer in Farsi,
while she paces
in the kitchen.

I pick up the phone
I pick up the phone
I pick up the phone

again,
make sure
the connection
is still good.

We each have our own
ways of praying.

After an Hour

Maman calls
the emergency department chief doctor.
The chief's wife is a patient of hers.
Maman delivered each of their three kids.

Phoenix is alive and okay.

The firework finale
booms and crackles.

We can visit him,
in the morning.

Fall Asleep Crying

Tears
burn salt into my face,
streak onto my neck,
spread across my upper lip.

The last things that lip touched
were Phoenix's lips.

I feel it again.
Air blown from my lungs into his—
as though it's happening right now.

Fear and hope
burn out
into finale smoke
and sleep.

Dream

I
blow air from my lungs into his
air from my lungs into his
from my lungs into his
my lungs into his
lungs into his
into his
his

Air
is a constant
firework finale we
share.

Between the Lungs (the Mediastinum) Sunday, July 5

Phoenix's parents talked with Maman,
said we could visit him at the hospital.

There's an X-ray up on the light box
across from his bed.

I see an arrow drawn on it
pointing to an area between the lungs.

Maman switches the light box on,
then quickly turns it off.

        Phoenix opens his eyes

        tells us

            the Hodgkin's lymphoma

        is back

        growing in his chest.

Maman whispers,
the mediastinum.

But

they can treat it, right?!
I ask.

Phoenix's voice sounds
hoarser than I remember.

> *Yeah, I'll have to be*
> *in the hospital*
> *twice this summer*
> *for the treatment.*

June gloom
hovers over
July.

Skeletal System

We're going to learn
the names of all the bones
in the med school for teens class.

I rest my tibia and fibula
on the empty chair in front of me.

We take notes.
We label diagrams.

When we get to the clavicle,
I can't stop writing it.
Over and over the same pen marks.

I can't move forward,
can't take more notes.

I need to recheck that I wrote
the whole word,
each letter.
Sound it out in my head.

I'm stuck.

Stuck in this cast.
Stuck in this class.
Stuck with being alone at home.

I just want to make Phoenix better.

He's like a spine.
Without him,
I don't know
if I'll be able
to stand.

My paper tears
where I've been writing
clavicle
over and over again,
at the
I.

When We Were Eight

I thought it was called the collarbone.

We were playing with his dog, Charlie.

As Phoenix bent down to pet Charlie,
he reached out with his hand
to grab the tennis ball out of Charlie's mouth.

I saw the lump.

Phoenix, what's that?

                                        What's what?

That bump
over your collarbone?

I reached out to touch it.

This.

Phoenix felt it.

                                        Oh—I don't know.
                                        Maybe I hit it against something.

Does it hurt?

                                        No.

Node

As Maman and I were leaving,
Phoenix's dad held
the front door open for us.
I remembered the lump.

I asked Phoenix's dad about it.

> *Where is the lump?*

I pointed to my collarbone.

He walked over to Phoenix and touched the lump.
Then he knelt down and felt all over Phoenix's neck.

He stopped and looked over at Maman,
scared.

Maman looked back with the same worried face.
She whispered.

> *Is it?*
> *A supraclavicular node?*

That's when
I found out,
the collarbone
is the *clavicle*.

It's where cancer can start.

Hodgkin's Lymphoma

The immune system
defends the body with cells
that patrol in the blood
and in our lymph nodes.

In Hodgkin's lymphoma,
the immune system is sick because
its B cell patrollers stop acting normally.

Instead of protecting,
they rebel and become the enemy.

Phoenix had Hodgkin's lymphoma.

For months, I couldn't play with him.

I missed him.

Nothing felt the same.

I Had to Do Something

One day I told Maman
I was going to go on a bike ride.

But instead, I went to Phoenix's bedroom window.
I gave him my mixed-up Rubik's Cube.

Want to solve this?

> *Oh, yeah!*
> *Thanks.*

When can we play again?

> *I just finished my last treatment.*
>
> *But when Mom and Dad*
> *talk at night,*
> *when they think I'm sleeping,*
> *I hear them say*
> *my tests don't look good.*

Oh.

> *They won't know for sure*
> *'til after my next test.*

Maman Made Āsh[12]   Saturday, March 6, 1982

She said we were going to take it to a friend's.

But we didn't get into the car.

She carried the pot out the front door,
told me to come with her.

We walked to Phoenix's.

> *Ava, you get to play*
> *with Phoenix today.*

Really!

> *His last tests looked good.*
> *Really good.*
> *He doesn't need*
> *any more treatments.*

> *We're having lunch to celebrate.*

Phoenix gave me
the solved Rubik's Cube.

> *I hid it in a box under my bed,*

he said as we giggled
and ate the āsh.

---

12. A thick Persian soup of noodles, lentils, beans, and herbs.

That day,
I figured it out.

Phoenix would be okay,
if I stayed close to him,

like that Rubik's Cube
he kept
under his bed.

Phoenix's Fourteenth Birthday   Tuesday, July 7, 1987

Maman makes āsh
for me to take to Phoenix's.

We blindfold Phoenix and
lead him out to the yard.

His new surfboard's wrapped
in a blue bow.

His mom takes the blindfold off
as we shout,

                                    Happy birthday!

He turns to all of us.
                    Thanks, everyone.
                    I can't wait to ride it.

With, Before Without

Phoenix goes
to the hospital today.

His parents pack the car.
He's going to start treatment.

Naz is here.
All the surfer dudes have also come over.

We all sit in the living room,
and listen to *The Joshua Tree.*

Tears Caught

Room 509 hands me his binder.
He has it open to a poem.

I start reading aloud,
but then I start to cry.

                              What happened?

Phoenix's cancer is back.

                              Who's Phoenix?

He's my
best friend.

                              Oh.
                              I'm sorry, Ava.

He fainted,
at the July Fourth Festival.

I had to give him mouth-to-mouth
while his dad pressed on his chest.

I ran after the ambulance.

I cry harder.
Tears drop onto the paper
in the binder.

Oh, I'm sorry,
I got your binder wet.

That's okay, Ava.
That's what that binder's for.

To catch tears—

Poems rise
up out of
falling tears.

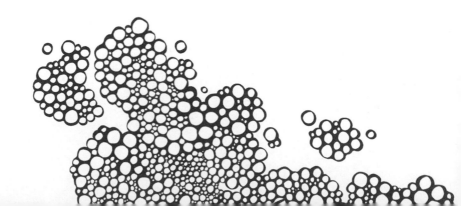

Window

Room 509 says:

I've read poems since I was a kid.

*As an orphan,
I moved around
from one foster home
to another.*

*Poems have
come to feel
like parents.*

*They see me
when it feels like
no one else can.*

*How about I
read a poem
for you today?*

Okay.

Keep knocking, and the joy inside
will eventually open a window
and look out to see who's there.[iv] —Rumi

Chemo

In the door
of his hospital room,
there's a little
window.

I peek through it.

Phoenix is in isolation.
The nurses say I can't go in.
His immune system's too weak.

He lays in the hospital bed.
I tap on the door.

He looks up,
then at me,
stares for a few
extra seconds.

I can see him mouth,

                    Hi.

I wave back.
He throws a shaka sign.

I throw one back with a smile.

Then he puts his hand up
like he is holding a mic.
Points at me with his other hand.

Maybe Bel told him
we're going to start
rehearsing tonight.

Hope

While I stare back at him,
all I can think about is hope.

He'll get to leave
in a few days.

He'll have one more treatment
next month.

Then he'll be done,
I hope.

All the bad cells knocked out by the chemo,
I hope.

Only the good ones will grow back,
I hope.

I raise my hand up like
I'm holding a mic.

I nod back,
Bye.

then wave.

Our First Rehearsal

Naz and Bel are going to perform
with me
at the Thanksgiving Concert on the Pier.

We meet at Naz's.
She'll play tumbak.

Bel will play guitar.

We need to learn
three cover songs.

We call our band
Ocean Drive.

Naz wants to cover the Bangles.
Bel wants to cover Madonna.

We decide to pick one from each.
We'll pick the third another time.

Hang Ten

Our visits are short,
but at least,
between
his treatments,
we can

listen
to music
way more
than we used to.

Phoenix reads *Surfer*
while I read liner notes.

He dog-ears pages,
cool shots
of huge waves.

I pull
the magazine away
from him.

What?!
Give that back.
I was reading that!

I never got to sign your yearbook,
since you skipped out
on our graduation party.
Sooo, I'm signing this.

"Hang ten!
Your best friend,
forever. Love, Ava"

Questions

But just after
I write it,
I realize
this is the first time
I've said or written
love
to Phoenix.

My face is on fire.

Why did I write love?
Is this love?
Like a brother, yes.
But Love?
What will he think
when he reads it?

Between

I bury
the magazine
in a pile

between

other
magazines.

I hope
he won't
look for it.

Otherwise
things

between

us won't
be the same.

*Ava, you know
what's about to happen!*

He throws his pillow at me
and laughs.
He reaches next to me
to grab the pillow,
he throws it again.
He reaches to grab it
for a third shot,
but I block
his arm.

My skin
tingles
                        between
where his hand
brushes my arm.

And all I want is
            for him to throw
                    the pillow again
                        and to let the pillow
                                fall next to me.
                        But I'm not sure
                his skin felt
        the same sparks
as mine.

He stops trying
for the pillow,
to catch his breath
                        between
our giggles
                        between
our fears.

July

When I'm not visiting Phoenix,

I'm on the pier
watching the waves
and the surfers.

I'm hearing sounds
I never used to,
as I sit still
in the movement
around me.

Shape and color,
shadow and curve
speak through,

the roll of a wave
        bobbing boards

                jumping over
                      diving in
                            seaweed and towels
                                  buckets and shovels

                hats and sandals,
                      scattered for miles.

A melody rises
        in my mind

da dada la da
da dada la da

Sneaker Wave

Like a sneaker wave
I didn't see coming,
the melody carries me.

It swallows
all of the shapes and colors
in its path.

It leaves
a single song.

And right now,

I'm the only one who knows how to hear it.
I'm the only one who knows how to ride it.
I'm the only one who knows how to sing it,

because it surges
with the beat
of my heart.

Ride the Melody Home

I

      drop
      my crutches,

            sit at the edge
            of my bed,

                        pick up
                        the guitar

            to find the
            matching chords.

     My ears
     hang ten

on the strings.

Shaken

While I walk on the pier,
one of my crutches gets stuck
in a crack between the wooden boards.

Someone grabs the crutch
and pulls it out of the crack.

I say thanks
before
I realize
it's volleyball guy
and he's not
giving
the crutch back.

He glances at the cast.
He points to Naz's dad's get well wish
written in Farsi.

Then volleyball guy fixes on my eyes
to stitch in some hate.

What happened?
You trip on a turban?!

A laugh explodes from his mouth
and the mouths of the boys walking with him.

He leans the crutch toward me.
I reach to take it
until he jams it back
into the crack
and walks away.

Rage fills my chest,
        pushes against my ribs,
                spills into my fists.

I want to swing my other crutch at him.
But everything would get worse
if I swung it.

So I stand
still,
like a shaken
can of soda.

Burst

At home
                           rage overflows
onto paper.

I can't help it.
I can't think of anything else.

My body's on my bed,
but it feels like I'm somewhere else.

My hand is holding a pen,
but if feels like it's also holding me.

Neat doesn't matter.
Order doesn't matter.

My heart beats
          through my fingers,
                    through the ink,
                              into freedom.

I write all the things
        I had wanted to say,
                all the thoughts,
                        even ones I didn't know,

the thoughts that hid
        beneath the feelings,
                the feelings that hid
                        beneath the thoughts.

Every word,
        like a geyser,
                rising with
                        power.

Last Stop Saturday, August 1

I bring a book
from home,
Rumi's poetry,
to lend to Room 509.

His room is
my last stop today.

But . . . his bed is empty.

Sheets are off.

Oh
my
God!

He's dead!

Transferred

Room 509's nurse says,

Honey, you okay?

She picks up
the Rumi book I dropped.

Room 509 . . . he's gone.

*Yeah, he was transferred to rehab,
on the second floor.*

Oh . . . I thought.

*Ava,
always ask the nurse.*

*That's one of the
most important things
to know about a hospital.*

She points to the stairs
that will get me to
the second floor.

Rehab

When I saw that your bed was empty,
I thought you were dead.

Silence, then he chuckles.

That is kind of funny though, isn't it?

No!

Ugh, okay, let's just forget about it.
You can give the book back to me
when you're done with it.

Thanks, Ava.

They thought I needed a little rehab,
so they moved me here.

He puts the book next to
his medications.
You forget to take your medicine?

Oh, no, I was waiting
for your reading.

Then I get to take the pill meds
with the word meds.

509 tells me a story.

Some trick when he was a kid,
about playing dead
with a friend from school.
He laughs.

His breathing gets easier
as he gets further into the story,
like when he's reciting a poem he's memorized
or when he listens to me read one to him.

Words are like medicine,
when the right ones are given,
and the right ones are heard.

Sneaking

Phoenix's last treatment
is tomorrow.

I'm supposed to be
learning about how the eyes (or ears?)
work tonight.

But I beg Maman
to let me skip class,
say I'm not feeling well,
say I'll study at home instead.

Then while she's in the bathroom,
I leave.

I run over to Phoenix's.
I put the mask
I stole from the hospital on.

His dad says, *Just fifteen minutes.*

The Third Song

Phoenix and Bel play Mario Brothers.
I sit down and Bel passes her controller to me.
Phoenix beats me.
They eat popcorn.

I tell them about how I thought 509 died.

I tell them about the seagull,
stuck in the snack shop.
How Naz and I got all this extra candy
'cause it was *contaminated.*
The store was going to throw it all away!

Bel shows me some chords on the guitar.
I start humming my new melody
I can't get rid of it.

What's that?

Phoenix asks.

What?

That song?

It's not a song.
It's something that just came to me.
It's been stuck in my head.

Bel starts playing chords to it.

She says,

Ava, we should play this for our third song
at the Thanksgiving Concert.

It's just a melody.

Can you write some words for it?

NO WAY.
We're gonna sing a cover.

Not my own
words.

Not my own
feelings.

Knocks on the Door

I hear
Maman's voice.

Phoenix's dad called Maman.
Told her I'd snuck over.

They say it's okay,
but I'll have to leave soon.

Bel and I hug.

I wave
to Phoenix.

Can't
risk him
getting exposed
to any germs.

But I still wish
I could
wrap my arms
around him too.

If I wrote

my own song lyrics
AND sang them,

I'd be afraid
to tell people of the parts
of me that feel broken
and the parts of my life
that still break me.

I'd be afraid that they'd see
there's no place
I really belong.

Not Persian enough at home.
Not American enough at the beach.
I don't have parents who stayed together.
There's no country or house that feels fully me.

Except, when
       Phoenix and I
              ride the waves.
                    A song I love
              plays on the radio.
       They tell me
I'm worth
every note
in the ocean.

Cast Off *Wednesday, August 5*

The doctor cuts through plaster.

I wish Phoenix's cancer

could be wrapped in a cast,

his blood cells set like bones.

Run to the Water

run run run
into the water
into the waves
hold my board

i   n   h   a   l   e

hold my breath
dive under

break
      swell
            paddle

e   x   h   a   l   e

      hard
            paddle
                 away

                      from casts and crutches
                      from badges and classes
                      from Maman and medicine
                      from my dad and distance
                      from hate and prejudice
                      from cancer and sickness

i   n   h   a   l   e

out back
beyond the break
sit on my board
cold water stings my ankle
cold water kisses my bones

e   x   h   a   l   e

Words I've known forever

but have never said
          break off of my tongue.

I hear them
                 for the first time.

The melody I'd caught
                    is the swell.

My words are the lip of the wave
               rolling into lyrics.

And my song
          barrels through with my heart.

We ride into the light.

Decorations

This classroom's like a throne for:
fluorescent lights,
prints of seaside villages,
faded and dated
wannabe impressionist
watercolor paintings,
windowless
walls,

like some of the patient rooms,
where the closest thing to music
is the beeps from drips and monitors,
pages overhead for extensions to dial
and code blues.

I wonder when
the med school for teens class
will explain
the decorations
here.

Structures of the Neck

I fill a page in the workbook
with doodles of the beach
and the words that came to me
while I was surfing.

The anatomy page
of the trachea and vocal cords
I cover with my own
vocal chords.

I write the lyrics

      over the diagram

            of where breath enters,

      they become a stream of stars

I can sing.

Keep Singing

Phoenix finished chemo.
He's back home,
recovering.

His golden hair is gone.

He wears the red beanie hat
that I threw at him,
last spring.

It looks like a fire
on his head.

He's thinner
than I've ever seen him.

Bel and I hang in the front yard.
Phoenix sits just inside
the open window,
tucked into a lounge chair.

I don't get too close.
I still can't expose
his weak immune system
to germs,
but we're close enough to talk.

I show my lyrics to Bel.

> *These are rad, Ava.*
> *We could totally play this.*

We practice together,
link her chords
with my melody and words.

Phoenix falls asleep.
I keep singing
like he's listening.

I hope he is.

Throwing Things

Maman sits on the couch,
eyes red and full of tears,
like a hurricane of
oceans coming out of her.

You're not happy here.
I'm obviously not enough for you.
Why don't you go
live with your baba?

What?

Maman opened my
med school for teens workbook.

She   *was curious*
about what we were learning.

She read what I wrote
about feeling alone,
out of place,
not understood.

Maybe you'll feel better there.

Maybe
I should.

But I
would never leave here,
the water,
Phoenix.

She
goes into the kitchen,
grabs a plate,
goes out onto the patio.

CRASH

White ceramic pieces roll
toward the grass.

I run to my room and
grab the door.

SLAM

Other People's Feelings

When I visit Room 509,
I see at least twenty pieces of paper,
with notes written on them,
sticking out of the Rumi book I lent to him.

Those are my favorites.
Can you find
the one marked "family"?

After I read one out loud for him,
I ask,

What was it like,
to not have parents?

It's all I knew.
It's all I know.

Did you want
someone to adopt you?

Yes, but
I was wishing for something
I didn't know.

Did you feel alone?

Yeah.

But then as I got older,
I saw that some of my friends
with parents,
well, they also felt alone.

Did people treat you like
you were weird?

Sometimes.
But eventually
I decided,
I didn't want to carry around
other people's feelings
about my life.

From His Dad

School starts in three weeks and two days.

Naz and I walk downtown from my place
to shop for clothes.

We see Phoenix
in his red cap
getting into his dad's car.

Hey Ava. Hey Naz.

Good to see you out, dude!
Naz says.

Where you headed?
I ask.

To the hospital,
to get some tests done and stuff,
every Monday for a bit.

You going to be able to start school with us?
I ask.

Phoenix looks at his dad.

I hope so,
his dad says, as he smiles
and pats Phoenix's back.

Phoenix gets his smirk from his dad.

More Doodles

It's the last night of
the med school for teens class.

Teacher's talking about blood cells.

Red, carry oxygen,
on hemoglobin.

White, fight invaders,
part of the immune system.

Claire's not paying any attention.
She's usually asking so many questions.

Unlike her to be doodling
and not taking notes.

Perspective

Phoenix's test results
looked good!

And so do the hospital halls today.

Now,
I see glimmers of hope.

Patients hoping
to get out,
to get better.

Other people
hoping for the patients too:
Cleaners
Transporters
Techs
Nurses and
Doctors,
hoping.

Now,
so am I.

Room 509 notices.

Says I skipped in.

> *I feel like skipping too.*
> *They say I get to leave in a few days.*

Oh!

> *What's in your step,*
> *something good?*

Phoenix
is getting better.

> *Oh good.*

> *Here.*

He passes the Rumi book
to me.

> *I haven't had time to remove*
> *my notes*
> *but don't want to forget getting this*
> *to you.*

That's cool.

So, this may be my last visit?

> *I think so.*

I read some poems from the binder to him,
ones I've read to him before.

But I guess like me and songs,
he likes hearing them again.

Maybe it's like what Maman says
about medicine.
You often need more than a dose
for it to have its full effect.

Summer's End

Naz trains the guy taking over for her at the snack shop.

My med school for teens class has an end-of-class party.
We get reflex hammers as gifts.

Every morning,
Naz, Bel, and I meet up
to play our songs.

Then we walk with Phoenix
to the sand

to watch the surf.

Paddle Out

The doctors
say Phoenix can finally
get in the water.

The horizon is so crisp,
you can understand why
some people thought they could
drop off
the edge of the earth.

While I wax our boards,
I see how loose Phoenix's wetsuit is.

His head turns white with sunblock
he and Bel are rubbing in on his bald head.

We paddle out,
duck under a wave,
settle away from
the other riders.

                                        The waves are cranking.

He sounds happy.

Yeah,
and clean.

Perfect for a
comeback.

For Today

Phoenix kicks and paddles hard.

He

        goes for a wave,

                holds on at the crest,

        cuts across the face,

rides just in front

        of the tube,

                drives through,

        does a cutback then

falls in.

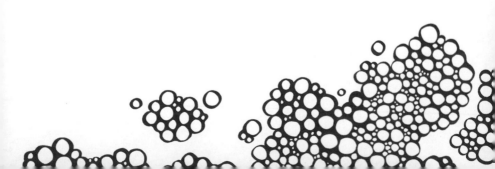

After he comes up,
he walks toward the sand
instead of heading back out.

He stands in the froth,
watches the water,
watches and watches it.

He looks back at me.
Gives me a thumbs up.
I send one back.

He's made
his comeback,
for today.

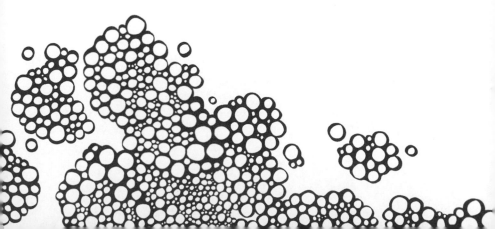

The Edge

Bel and I bury Phoenix under the warm sand.

Naz gets us slushies from the shop.

We wait and watch

while surfers watch and wait

on an edge

they want to ride

over.

Pick Up Our Schedules

Naz and I get Algebra together.

Claire walks into the office.

Hey Claire.
Why is she here?

You going to
go to school here?

                                        Hi.

                                        Yeah.
                                        We just moved into this district.

Naz says,
                    You should sit with us
                    for lunch tomorrow.

                                        Cool. Thanks.

While we walk away,
I shove my elbow into Naz
and whisper, *Really?*

He Won't

I take Phoenix's schedule to his place.

His dad answers the door.

Eyes

      red.

            Phoenix

      won't

start school
tomorrow.

His test results weren't good,
his dad says.

The tumor
in Phoenix's chest has

      grown.

First Day of Ninth Grade   Wednesday, September 9

I'm in class
with a crack in my heart.

The only thing
I want to do

is to cut the cancer
out of him

and be
at his house.

Locker

After class,
I can't get away
from my locker.

Do I have the right
books and binders?

Triple-check.
Lose count of the checks.
Start over.

Every time I close the locker door,
I have to open it again,
to see if I left anything
behind.

open
scan
close

open
scan
close

open
scan
close

blue english
red math
yellow history

blue english
red math
yellow history

blue english
red math
yellow history

1, 2, 3 binders
1, 2, 3 binders
1, 2, 3 binders

I count the books.
But I am not really counting.

My mind is locked
onto Phoenix.

Fill

Fill the crack in my heart.
Fill the gap of not knowing.

Fill them with counting,
to be certain,
sure of
what's in front of me.

But I'm not.

What I Need

Naz comes over.

You okay?

Phoenix is worse.

No.

She sees I'm stuck
staring into the locker.
She places her fingers on my chin.

Ava.

She turns my head
away from the books and binders.

She closes the locker.
She puts her arm around my shoulders
and nudges me to walk away.

I'm not sure if I have
what I need
for class,

but I know I have
what I need
from Naz.

Ms. Rivers invited
me, Naz, and Bel
to play
what we've been rehearsing
for her.

When we're done, she says:

Naz and Bel,
the tumbak and guitar sound great.

Ava, it's good to hear you
using your voice.

Ava, I know your Festival prize was
for a private lesson.
But what do you think about
using it to prep all of you
for the Thanksgiving Concert?

Yeah, that would be good, Ms. Rivers.
Thank you, I say.

She tells us to meet her
every Thursday after school.

She'll wait
for me and Naz
to ride over
to the junior high.

Naz and Bel high-five.

Intersection

The light turns green.

Naz and I start pedaling
our bikes across the street.

                                        Hey!

Someone shouts from
the cars to our right.

                                        Hey!
                                        Hermositas!

A guy yells
as he sticks his head out
over a car window.

We hear a whistle, two notes,
as we pump harder.

We get away as fast as we can.
We head to Naz's.

Her mom puts my bike
in the back of their station wagon . . .

                    He thought you two were Latinas?

and gives me a ride home.

Extended Family Dinner Friday night, September 11

Uncle Rāmīn pops in with *Cheh khabar!*
—he hollers it out as he steps
through the front door.

He pinches my cheeks like he did when I was five.
The cigarette he just smoked is my new perfume.

Cheh What   *khabar* news

School   It's all new.
                         At the end of the day,
                         my head is spinning.
                         Even though most of what I've done
                         is sitting.

Performance   Naz and Bel and I
                         need to get
                         three songs ready.
                         One of them I wrote,
                         and Maman doesn't
                         exactly love the lyrics.

Words   Strangers say
                         I don't belong and
                         things that are so
                         warped.

My dad   The only kind of dad I know
                         is the kind you don't live with,
                         the kind that, even if I asked why,
                         has answers that wouldn't be enough.

Maman	She thinks
	music isn't worth the time
	and that being a doctor is the best.
	But I think
	the nurses and staff don't get enough credit.
	Hospitals seem a bit inhuman.
	The art is sad and there's no music.
	And for all the *fixing* Maman says it does,
	medicine hasn't healed Phoenix.

Phoenix	My best friend's cancer's back.
	He's getting worse.
	And I need him alive,
	more than anything.

| *Cheh* | *khabar!* |
| I holler back. | |

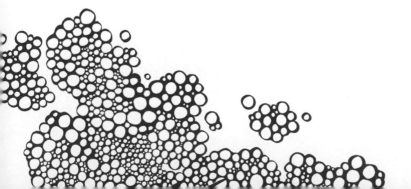

We are the night ocean filled
with glints of light. We are the space
between the fish and the moon,
while we sit here together.[v] —Rumi

Fourteen Years

Heat wave.
Santa Ana winds.

We bring our beach chairs
instead of our boards.

Bel runs over.

> *Happy Birthday, Ava!*

Thanks, Bel.

She runs toward the water
with her boogie board.

Phoenix turns to me.

> *Man, fourteen years.*
> *How does it feel?*

You know.
You've been fourteen
since July.

Phoenix turns back
to look at the water.

Well,
if you really want
to know,
it feels
I'm gonna be honest
like maybe I don't . . .

He looks back at me.

                                   You don't what?

I can feel my eyes fill.
I can't hold it in anymore.

Like I don't belong
here.

Here Now

No one really wanted me
when I was born.
I was
a mistake.

> *A mistake?*
> *Your mom loves you.*

My dad wasn't
even there.

> *You're not a mistake.*

My family,
their country,
our language—
people make fun of them,
of me.

> *They're idiots.*

It doesn't feel like
I belong.

> *You belong, here, now.*

I look away.

> *Are you even hearing*
> *me?*

The water's choppy.

Ava, you're here, now
with all of us.

I look down at the sand.

You're here, now,
with all of this.

This sand has never cared
how I got to it.

You're here now with . . .

I grab a handful of sand,
watch it fall through . . .

me.

Turning

His hand touches my shoulder.

I turn my head back toward him.

He's so close to me that his lips glide just past mine

as he reaches around me into a hug.

I can feel warm air from his nose on my neck.

I

b   r   e   a   t   h   e   i   n ,

            him,

b   r   e   a   t   h   e   i   n ,

                me,

b   r   e   a   t   h   e   i   n ,

                    here,

b   r   e   a   t   h   e   i   n ,

                        now.

b   r   e   a   t   h   e   i   n ,

                    Every wave,

b   r   e   a   t   h   e   i   n ,

            alone or in a set,

b   r   e   a   t   h   e   i   n ,

            rises from

b   r   e   a   t   h   e   i   n ,

the sea.

Breathing

The best birthday gift.
It's not a thing, but feeling
I'm right here, breathing.

At Rehearsal

Something's changed.

More power
in my voice.

Not wondering,
if being different
is not belonging,
if being alone
has to be lonely.

I may not belong
in the way the TV says, but
I belong
from where I came, and
I belong
to where I am.

The sand I decide to hold
is up to me,
and so is what I sing.

The song

holds me

until I

become

the rise,

the reach,

the crest,

the crescendo

of seas,

my crash

and roar,

once seen,

once heard,

I can

never unknow,

how water

breathes

my song.

Make a Stop

Bel and I ride our bikes
to the candy shop
on the way home.

In the distance,
at the outdoor tables,
a girl with a guy.

He's wearing a red cap.

We get closer.
It's Phoenix,
with Claire.

Sweat drips down my arm and neck.

Why is she?
Here?

Jealousy:
the fear
of nothing I
expect.

Old Place, New Person

Hi, Ava!

Hey Claire,
I say.

Bel hugs Phoenix.
I hug him,
a bit longer than normal,
for Claire to see.

I get money out of my wallet.
Pretend to not care.

I try to focus on the bills
but can't read the numbers.
Like I'm blind.

How's it going, Claire?
Bel's not blind.

How do you know each other?
I ask.
Bel looks at Phoenix.

Claire's new at school,
Phoenix says.

I know,
but you
haven't
been to school?

More sweat drips down my side.

> *We met at the hospital.*
> *I'd fill the snacks*
> *in the chemo waiting room*
> *as part of my volunteer work.*
> *Phoenix was there sometimes,*
> *during his treatments,*
> Claire says.

Bel looks at me and says,
> *Claire told us she just moved here.*
> *We told her we'd show her the snack shop.*

Cool.
Not.

I was hot
like vinyl car seats in August
and I'm wearing shorts.

I sit down in a chair
and I'm getting burned.

Swerve

After school,
she doesn't know it,
but I ride my bike
behind Claire on hers.

She turns left.
I turn right.

I can't forget
that she was there
with Phoenix and
something wasn't said.

HONK!
I swerve
around a car
as I make
a U-turn.

Follow her

from just far enough behind.
She rides into an apartment complex.

My fingers are cold.
My stomach flutters.

I tiptoe my bike in.
        My legs
                can't be stopped.

Her bike is locked at the second set of steps.

I lower my bike slowly,
        lay it on the ground.
        I sneak up like I
                can't be stopped.

I'm looking for
        what wasn't said.
        I don't know
        what I'll find.

But I know how I feel
        about Phoenix
                can't be stopped.

Side Yard

Her shoes are at the front door.
She's inside.

Maybe I could just
stand here and listen.

No! I turn.
This is dumb.

                                   Ava?

Too late.
I turn back.

She was in
the side yard
that I didn't see.

Claire!

                                   You okay?

I . . .

                                   Want to come in?

Okay.
No.

Behind the Front Door

Want something to drink?

She runs to the kitchen.

Do you like lemonade?

Sure.

I stand in the entry

by the wall

filled with framed photographs:

crawling baby, Claire
hanging upside down on monkey bars, Claire
double Dutch jump roping, Claire
balance-beaming gymnastics, Claire
medal around her neck, Claire
between her parents, the Grand Canyon cliffs behind, Claire

baseball cap–wearing, pale, thin, eating ice cream, Claire
smiling wide, on a Ferris wheel, bald, Claire

She finds me

still staring
at the wall.

> You wondering
> what happened
> to my hair?

But I know.
Look at her
like I don't.

> That's when I
> was on chemo.

Oh.

For . . .

> lymphoma.

She hands me

the lemonade.

I felt worse.

But I needed

to know where

Phoenix

and she

became friends.

So you . . . ?

at the hospital?

He promised.

Not even me.

I know what it's like

to feel different.

No,
but some people act
like another culture is
a cancer.

I got better.

But I wanted

to be somewhere where

no one knew

I had had cancer,

didn't treat me

like I was pitiful.

So when I met Phoenix in the
support group,

I asked him

not to tell anyone

about it.

You?

You had . . . ?

Lemonade

Claire got better from her cancer.

We stare at the photos.

> *I loved my doctors.*
> *I want to care for kids*
> *like my doctors cared for me.*

That's why she liked our class.

The class was my mom's idea.
She thinks I should be a doctor.

We sip lemonade
between the stories.

Bitter getting sweet.

My dad mails

a birthday gift to me,
a cassette recorder
and some blank
Memorex tapes.

His
present
is late,
as usual.

And he thinks
presents
are a kind of
presence.

Mixtaping

Click a new blank tape into the slot.
Cue the tape to the black.
You can't record on the clear part.

Have the radio on whenever
you're in your room.
Keep the recorder close to the radio speakers.

Press record as soon as you hear the DJ announce the song.
Pray he doesn't speak past the intro.

Stay as quiet as you can while the song plays.
Press stop when the song is done.

You might record part of a commercial.
That's okay.

You can record silence
over that part.

Rewind, make sure you got the recording.

Play the tape for a few extra counts
after the end of the song
to cue the tape for the next recording.

There needs to be some quiet,

between the
songs
to make a good set.

You'll have to record over some songs,
because the phone rings or
because Maman walks into your room
to tell you it's time for dinner.

That's okay.
You'll hear the song on the radio again.

It'll take a few weeks to fill the tape.

It's definitely okay
if the recording picks up
the sound of the play button
getting clicked down.

Those are some of the best sounds.
Like water splashing
as you paddle for a wave,

the ride's about to start.

Confession

Words recorded on the tape
don't say it.

And neither can I
yet.

But the songs pulse
from my heart

at the rate of
love.

I write on the label:
For Phoenix, love Ava

Fall
1987

Meet Up

As I head to his house,
I can see Phoenix
through the front window.

Headphones on
over his red beanie,
eyes closed,
he's somewhere else,
until I knock.

He opens his eyes
and takes his headphones off.

I don't remember his wrist looking,
or my breath feeling,
so thin.

On the walk

to the beach
he catches me up.

School at home's going okay.
I go in for some tests tomorrow
and the support group.
And

And?

Claire said
you
followed her home.
Found out about her.

Yeah, sorry,
I messed that secret up.

Not sure I should forgive you.

He smiles.
I look down.

But I get it, you were

curious   *jealous.*

I smirk,
still looking down,
while I squeeze the mixtape
in my sweatshirt pocket.

Overhead

The waves are overhead today.

*You're gonna be so stoked when
you get out there again.*

I don't know.

What?

I

What?

I'm just.

*You have to
keep fighting,
Phoenix.*

You think I'm not?

I don't know anymore.

*Do you think I get to decide?
If—*

*No.
But maybe if I
could do something.*

*You think you can
stick your hand out
and the wave won't
break over it?*

No, but I can stay
with the wave.
I can hold on to it.

Phoenix looks away.

I can't feel my legs.
Your mom and dad need you.

My throat is knotted.
Bel needs you.

I fall to the sand.
I
need you.

Phoenix kneels down next to me.
So you keep holding on too.

Here.
I made this for you.

I press the mixtape
into his chest,

>   like it's the needle on a syringe
>   filled with a cure,

>   like those songs will
>   choke the cancer,

>   because love invades spaces
>   death doesn't know how to reach.

Making Sure

Phoenix

        wraps my hand with both of his hands,

Right then I know.

              takes the tape,

I'm going to keep making tapes.

                 reads the label,

I'm not going to miss a walk.

                     looks at me like a sunrise,

Not a single day.

              puts the tape in his pocket,

I'm going to be his hope.

         keeps a hand over the tape

Make sure he doesn't let go.

      as we walk back home.

I'll stay.

Blank Tape

After school,
I slide a new blank tape into the recorder
just for me to practice my song
for the Thanksgiving Concert.

Ms. Rivers said to try to
sing it in different ways,
change my volume and phrasing.

But questions keep invading
my brain.

What if volleyball guy is in the crowd?
What if Maman starts crying in the crowd?
What if my voice gets way off-key?

But Phoenix will be in the crowd.
He's like this tape, holding my story.

I'll just keep my eyes on him
to remind me I'm okay.

Bel's not

at rehearsal.

Run through our parts without guitar.
Barely say goodbye to Naz.

Race my bike to
Bel and Phoenix's.

Swollen faces.
Splotchy cheeks.

Test results:
The cancer's worse.

He'll just

go in for some extra treatments.
It's okay.
He's gotten better before.
He can fight this off.

Ava,

his mom says,

I think Phoenix doesn't want
any more treatments.

Yeah,
I remember,
there's the experimental one I heard about.
That's what he'll do next, right?

I turn to Phoenix's dad.
Bel is crying in his arms.

He shakes his head.

Ava, he doesn't want to go through it anymore.

On the coffee table,
a pamphlet's open.

"What to expect from hospice[13] care."

---

13. A kind of medical care that focuses on comfort at the end of life.

Stop, Drop, and Roll

Stop, Stop, Stop
Everyone is giving up.

Drop, Drop, Drop
I'll fall in.
"Where is he?!"

                                          With the support group,

his mom says.

                                          They decided to meet early,
                                          for Phoenix.

Roll, Roll, Roll
My feet punch
at the bike pedals,

aim at the hospital.

Bike pedals punch back

when my bike wheels hit
a bump in the road.

I'm thrown
over handlebars.

Cut my head.

Grind my palms
and knees
into asphalt.

Red and white sirens,
the color of blood
      and surrender,
take me home,
and scream out:
      I won't see Phoenix
      tonight.

Phone Call from Phoenix

Hey Ava.

Hey Phoenix.

*I heard about what happened,
your fall.
You okay?*

*I heard about
your . . .*

*No,
I'm not okay!*

Ava, the cancer's worse.

I know, but—

*It's growing
inside my chest.
It's so hard for me
to catch
my breath.*

*Don't you want to try
everything possible
that might help
you live?*

*I have.
And any more of it
feels like I'm
giving away any life
I have left.*

But I can help.
I can make sure—

I don't want to hurt anymore.
I don't want to throw up anymore.
Sometimes, it feels like I am
sucking air in through a straw.

My throat drowns
in a monster swell
of lost hope.

I look at the picture
of our kindergarten class
on my dresser.
I stare at the image of Phoenix,
blurry through my tears.

My voice surfaces.

Love.
I whisper.

I touch the image of his face
in the picture.

I . . . love . . . you.

His throat is drowning too.
But his voice swims.

I love you too, Ava.

Phoenix.

I'll see you
tomorrow.

Dinner at My House

Fisinjūn[14] and tahdīg[15]
—Phoenix's favorites.

Maman made them just for him.
Maman invited him, Bel, and their parents over for dinner.

I can't speak.

I set the table,
check the place settings
check the place settings
check the place settings.

Phoenix says there's nothing more the treatments can do.
He's tired of blood draws, vomiting, pain, and foggy thoughts.
He's ready to live as much as he can until—.

We're all sobbing.

Then I see his mom
smile when he says,

> *I'm going to surf*
> *and play guitar*
> *and hang with my friends.*

He looks at me.
I can't speak.

---

14. A stew of chicken mixed with a creamy sauce of ground walnuts and pomegranate syrup.
15. "Bottom of the pot" in Farsi. A crispy, buttery rice layer, which could include thinly sliced potatoes and saffron, made by panfrying the bottom of a pot of rice.

He's forgetting,
like I forgot about Olive.

He's letting go, like Maman and my dad
let go of each other.

But I can show him,
show all of them,
show me,
I won't give up.

My hope will fight his cancer away.

Just to be held by the ocean is the best luck
we could have.[vi] —Rumi

Beach Days

I visit Phoenix every day after school.
Walk with him to the water.
Set up beach chairs.

For a few weeks,
he surfs.
Takes waves in the smaller sets.
We listen to a mixtape.
I make a new one every week.

For a few weeks,
I carry the board to the foam.
He paddles out and rides the water,
after the wave breaks,
like a boogie boarder.
He doesn't pop up on his board.

The surfer crowd from school starts hanging with us more.
Same with Naz and Bel and Claire.

One day

he decides
not to go into the water.

We set the beach chairs
right at the water's edge.

Everyone sits around him.

We get soaked,
over and over,
hollering,
and laughing,
and splashing each other.

Phoenix is laughing
the hardest.

Rays

Hope
is watching an ocean's skyline
with Phoenix.

Hope
is our feet getting wet
as we walk on the shore.

Hope
is skin soaked by the ocean
and its stories of curling
around icebergs and lava fire,
lush cliffs and coral reefs.

Hope
is our eyes set
on the sun being hidden,
rays more beautiful
when they're broken.

Hope
is me staying close to Phoenix,
reminding him
there's still light in the sky
when the world turns dark.

Let the beauty we love be what we do.
There are hundreds of ways to kneel and kiss the ground.[vii] —Rumi

Until

He can't go to the beach today.

He's staying in the
downstairs bedroom now,

his mom says.

I set the folded beach chairs
down near the bedroom door.

He's in the bed,
sitting up against pillows.

He opens his eyes as I walk in.
He points to his guitar.

I hand it to him.

His playing

    sounds like

        praying.

            Ava,

                I'm so stoked

                    I got to

                        hear your

                            song.

                        The waves

                    we caught

                together

            made

        my life

    so beautiful,

like you.

Sandcastle Made of Hope

Phoenix's mom, Bel, and Naz
walk in
holding slushies.

We sip on them together
until Phoenix falls asleep.

His mom gives me a hug.

He hadn't played guitar
in a few days.

Thanks for coming by.

I start to build a sandcastle,
in my mind.

Phoenix helped me finish one
when we were little,
that day we became friends on the beach.

This time, I'm going to help him with his.
This time, it'll be made of grains of
not
giving
up.

I'm not supposed to be here   Friday night, November 20

hiding under Phoenix's bed.
Maman thinks I'm staying
over at Naz's house.

Phoenix is so sick though.
I snuck in through the window,
crawled by his guitar.

I need to

hear his breathing,
remind him of the waves.
We still have more to carve.

Stay close.

Make sure

my best friend
won't

die.

Holding Hands

While his mom and dad pore over
hospice nurse notes and lukewarm tea
at the kitchen table,
I inch across the floor to the edge of the bed.

Wrap my hand around his palm.

Whisper,

Phoenix, you're
             gonna get better. We're here. Your mom and dad, Bel,
                      and me. I get to sing "Wave" *at the concert*
                               next week. You'll stand with your board,
                      in the crowd, to calm my nerves,
             remind me of what we say
when we're surfing,

"If you don't take the
                          d
                          r
                          o
                          p

you miss the
                          r
                               i
                          d
                             e."

Feathers from My Throat

I sing to remind him
of us in the water.

I can't feel time
      in the melody.
            Song lines out
                  of my mouth
          are bird wings
      slamming my heart
just before

                        the bird soars . . .
                          we get to ride.

His hand grasps mine
      I climb out from
          under the bed.
             Ache and hope
        pull my lips, I beg,
    Phoenix, I need you.
I can't . . . Don't go.

Set

I

e

s   *e*

     you.

I

e

s   *e*

     me.

i *d*

R   *e*

    with

     me.

Full

My head falls
onto his chest.

His heart pulses
the sky into mine.

I feel beats,
the flutter of wings.

I fill my arms
with him,

then I slide back
under the bed.

Dawn

Blue light frames the curtains.
Soft music streams from the boom box.

The door is open.

I fell asleep.

I can hear Bel,
Phoenix's mom and dad,
all crying
in the other room.

My heart starts banging on my brain.

But I was here.
He couldn't have . . .

He's

gone.

The Guitar

I grab his guitar.

      I fill my arms with it.

            We climb

                  out of the window,

            run toward the water.

Run
        Hold
Run
        Hold
Run
        Hold
            Run
                Hold
                    Fold
                        Curl
                    Round
              Slap
            Burst
        Scream
    Shout

      o
R   r
          a

Run

I
tumble
onto
the
sand,
an
ocean
of
sorrow
rushes
through
me,
into
earth.
I
let
it
run.

My Front Door

Maman opens it.
She's half asleep.

What happened?

Our eyes meet.

She holds me
like she hasn't held me
in a while.

I let her,
like I haven't let her
in a while.

Friend

Phone rings.

Maman calls out,

> *Ava, the phone's for you.*
> *It's Naz.*

I pick up.

> *Ava?*

Naz . . .
he

> *Coming.*

Just Sit

Maman makes hot tea.

Naz and I sip
and sit
in my room.

I took his guitar.

Naz says,

> *He would've wanted
> you to have it.*

Bel walks in,

> *Naz's right.
> He would've wanted
> you to have it.*

Bel hugs me tight.

> *The funeral's Friday.*

Listen and See

Naz turns on the boom box.

She plays the Cure,
"Just Like Heaven."

Rewinds and plays it
over and over.

We sit.
We listen.

Naz says,

> *Bel, I'm not sure we should*
> *still perform*
> *at the concert on Saturday?*

Bel says,

> *For sure, we should.*
> *He'd be mad if we didn't.*

We sit.
We listen.

I close my eyes
and see

Phoenix.

He drops

   down the face

      of a wave.

        He carves

         his ride,

       long and free.

      Then we dance,

   deep beneath

the waves.

Go

Dresser top,
disorganized:
earrings out,
necklaces tangled,
tapes
out of their cases,
frames
not lined up.

Get up.
Straighten the frames.

Catch myself
in the mirror.
Eyes swollen and
red.

A voice
in my ear,
*Don't give away
any life
you have left.*

*Take the drop.
Ride.*

I change my clothes.
I grab my board
and go.

Thanksgiving, Persian Style

Thursday, November 26

We're at Uncle Rāmīn's this year.

> Turkey
> Green beans
> > —seasoned with butter and turmeric
> Potatoes
> > —cooked thin and crisp under rice, as tahdīg
> Beef kabob skewers
> Pita bread
> Red currant rice
> Whole milk yogurt
> > —with cucumber and dill

Set the table at seven p.m.,
two hours after the invitation time.

Bel and her parents are with her grandparents tonight.

I won't have to pass tea 'cause we're not at my house.
But I'll still drink in some stares from the Armani ladies.

I wear my red corduroy miniskirt 'cause
red was Phoenix's favorite color.

One of the Armani ladies walks toward me
and speaks in my ear.

I love your skirt.
When I was in Iran,
in university,
twenty years ago,
I wore one just like it.

My Maman buzurg[16]
hated it.
I didn't care.
I miss that skirt.

Then she kisses me,
Persian style,
a kiss on each cheek.

As she walks away,
she shouts in the air,
           āfarīn![17]

16. Grandmother.
17. Farsi for "Well done!" .

Today, like every other day, we wake up empty
and frightened. Don't open the door to the study
and begin reading. Take down a musical instrument.[viii] —Rumi

Alone in My Room

After the funeral,
streaks of powdered salt
crack over my cheeks.
My eyes are sore and burning.

I touch the guitar body,
smooth and cool.
I wrap my hand
around the neck.

If I plucked a string,
would it be like
he was speaking to me?
And I'd speak back,
but could he hear it?
Would it
break me more?

I haven't held it since
the day he died.

But now,
I need
to hold
what he held.

I pick it up.
I wrap my arm around it.
My hands hover
over the strings.

Strum

Left hand
fingers
A major.

Right hand
strums.

low
        to
                high
                high
        to
low

hello,
        good
                bye
                hello
        good
bye

three
        notes
                turn
                into
        a
smile

Gratitude

for

the waves
his hands made,

          shaping castles and
          sharing slushies,

          strumming these guitar strings,
          paddling over a swell,

          making sets of them,
          when his hand held mine.

How when he called my name,
it felt like home.

How when a steel string is pulled,
like memories,
a song breaks free,
to rise,
to fly.

I move
the wings.

Without

the movement
the change
the up and down
the rise and fall
the love and loss
the breath in then out
the full and then the empty
the empty ready to be filled

—just strings
that would never
shape a note or play
a song.

The universe and the light of the stars come through me.[ix] —Rumi

Thanksgiving Concert on the Pier

I bring Phoenix's guitar.
Bel said,

> *Just in case.*

Naz, Bel, and I meet behind the stage.
Run through the songs.

We set up and do a sound check
during the last hula hoop contest.

They award the pie contest winner.
The elementary school choir performs.

Maman runs backstage
to give me an old jam jar

filled with hot tea.

> *You'll need this.*

Then, It's Our Turn

After the first two covers,
the crowd cheers.

My hands are sweating so hard now.
We've only played "Wave" for Ms. Rivers.

I see her in the crowd.
She nods her head.

Bel puts her mouth to my ear.
I can't play this one with you.

What?
I don't know all of the chords!

She looks at Naz,
then hands a tape
to the sound guy.

Before I can say anything to her,
I hear a guitar playing.

It's the chords to "Wave."

Bel hands me Phoenix's guitar.

The sound guy announces:

Ladies and gentlemen,
for this song,
in place of Bel playing guitar—
her brother,
Phoenix!

Take the Drop

I lift the guitar up,
the sound of his name
still ringing in my ears.

Pull the strap over my head,

i   n   h   a   l   e.

Then I take the   d
                         r
                         o
                         p.

I strum to the tape.
             I sing with the chords,
                    like the notes are waves
                          landing on a shore.

This breaking wave
             will sound
                like this,
                    just once.

But I'll hear my voice
             surf this song,
                our hands play,
                    evermore.

His guitar strums
             and my song
                carry me
                    home.

Connect

I open my eyes
and see
a girl in the crowd
who says with her eyes,
she's felt the same.

And from her,
into me,
pours connection.

I am seen —She is seen.

I am heard—She is heard.

Singing My Own Song

My voice,

it is

a newborn blanket

wrapped around my

shaking arms and legs.

I'm held up onstage.

The crowd cheers

a tidal wave.

"Welcome

to the world."

I am enough.

Now.

Always.

Ava.

Circle

Backstage,
we form a circle.

Maman,
the Skylers,
me and Naz.

We

                    hold

                    each

other.

We're all displaced.
Maman from Iran,
me from my dad,
all of us from Phoenix.

We find home
in each other,
in what we've shared,
in this moment,
in right now.

Breathe Color

I take the Rumi book
off my shelf.

I turn to a page Room 509
marked,
Breathe.

The morning wind spreads its fresh smell.
We must get up and take that in,
that wind that lets us live.
Breathe before it's gone.[x]

I see another note,
marked,
Color.

Walk out like someone suddenly born into color.[xi]

On the Water

Swirling blue-green
            seaweed laced

    W   V   S
          A   E

each **whirlucent** one

        a chance to

                watch
                        hope
                            crest
                                drop
                                    carve
                                        hold
                                            ride
                                                love
                                            breathe
                                        slip
                                    fall
                                rise
                        fly
                    find
                light
        sing

a **song**

            that will take me all

                        the way to

                                the **shore**.

WAVE

I want to run right out of here,
make the pain disappear.
Leave the promises behind,
what they say I should be.

I want to belong like stars to night
but hate hides all the light.
Some say they care, but they're blind
to the galaxies behind these eyes.

CHORUS:
But when we ride the waves
and tumble beneath the break,
rise into the light,
breathe in every ray.
So I'll take the drop.
The whirlucent tide,
we get to ride,
we get to ride.

We fly on turns of salt and blue,
water glows and soaks right through.
I see us in those rolling tubes.
Holding hands with the moon.

Today the sun burns in the sky.
I'll ask Earth not to turn away.
But I can see fire wings take shape—
We carve our own way.

And when we ride the waves
and tumble beneath the break,
rise into the light,
breathe in every ray.
So I'll take the drop.
The whirlucent tide,
we get to ride,
we get to ride.

Fall into the flow and hear
all the songs it sings.
We belong like every wave
belongs to the sea.

Fall into the flow and hear
what you're worth; it's every note.
Like water, reach without the fear,
to the shore.

Like when we ride the waves
and tumble beneath the break,
rise into the light,
breathe in every ray.
So I'll take the drop.
The whirlucent tide,
we get to ride,
we get to ride.

(Outro)
To the light.
There I see you.
There I see me.

Phoenix to Ava

	SONG	ARTIST
1	Bizarre Love Triangle	New Order
2	King for a Day	Thompson Twins
3	(Forever) Live and Die	Orchestral Manoeuvres in the Dark
4	Trip Through Your Wires	U2
5	Ask	The Smiths
6	True Colors	Cyndi Lauper
7	Stand by Me	Ben E. King
8	She Sells Sanctuary	The Cult
9	But Not Tonight	Depeche Mode
10	Don't Dream It's Over	Crowded House
11	Life's What You Make It	Talk Talk
12	Stay	Oingo Boingo
13	Here Comes the Sun	The Beatles

Ava
to
Phoenix

	SONG	ARTIST
1	Something So Strong	Crowded House
2	Don't Get Me Wrong	Pretenders
3	Mad About You	Belinda Carlisle
4	In Your Eyes	Peter Gabriel
5	The Tide Is High	Blondie
6	Livin' on a Prayer	Bon Jovi
7	Shadows of the Night	Pat Benatar
8	Broken Wings	Mr. Mister
9	Lean on Me	Club Nouveau
10	If You Leave	Orchestral Manoeuvres in the Dark
11	With or Without You	U2
12	Bye Bye Pride	The Go-Betweens
13	Just Like Heaven	The Cure

Jalāl al-Dīn Rūmī
(1207–1273)
often referred to as Rumi, was a Persian poet, Sufi mystic, theologian and teacher, who created the physical meditation practice of whirling. He is considered one of the greatest Persian poets.

Endnotes

i. Coleman Barks, trans., *The Essential Rumi* (San Francisco: HarperCollins, 1995), 70 *(see page iv)*
ii. Ibid, 69 *(see page 4)*
iii. Ibid, 46 *(see page 151)*
iv. Ibid, 101 *(see page 180)*
v. Ibid, 260 *(see page 238)*
vi. Ibid, 105 *(see page 275)*
vii. Ibid, 36 *(see page 278)*
viii. Ibid, 36 *(see page 297)*
ix. Ibid, 138 *(see page 302)*
x. Ibid, 267 *(see page 308)*
xi. Ibid, 22 *(see page 308)*